# All Due To Reilly

Amber Jo Illsley

BALBOA.
PRESS
A DIVISION OF HAY HOUSE

Balboa Press books may be ordered through booksellers or by contacting:

Balboa Press
A Division of Hay House
1663 Liberty Drive
Bloomington, IN 47403
www.balboapress.com.au
1 (877) 407-4847

Print information available on the last page.

ISBN: 978-1-4525-2900-4 (sc)
ISBN: 978-1-4525-2901-1 (e)

Balboa Press rev. date: 06/12/2015

# CONTENTS

# CHAPTER ONE

## *Them's The Breaks*

The air on the West Coast of New Zealand's South Island fairly crackled with vibrancy after a night of heavy rain. The new day had turned into sunshine and the scent of the nearby sea was intoxicating, so much so that my cats were cavorting around outside as if the fresh new day had been their own successful invention.

I experienced that wonderful feeling of "heartswell" while watching the cats, Seamus O'Reilly and Katie O'Brien (Reilly and Katie for short) with coats glistening with health, playing all sorts of cat games. Their dexterity, combined with their obvious joy in their play was a vision, rather than music, to soothe the savage breast. My breast is rarely savage, but if it was, I'm sure that the vision of cat antics would soothe it no end.

A vehicle came up my driveway to the small cottage I rented at Carter's Beach, a few kilometres from Westport. My friends Kevin and Shelley exited from their four-wheel drive Lada and came inside for a cup of coffee and a chat. They are two of the most adventurous and amusing people I know, and so any conversation with them is bound to be stimulating.

As we chatted I was aware of Reilly sniffing around the wheels of their vehicle, and although I knew Reilly didn't normally go into dog mode and lift his leg against a wheel, he is such an interesting cat that nothing he did would surprise me anymore. In other words, he *has* very much surprised me over the few years since he first deigned to share his life with me.

Reilly stared up at the bonnet of the Lada, weighing the distance, and with a sudden leap, he bounded up there and then on to the roof of the cottage, landing with a great thump.

"What on earth was that?" Shelley exclaimed.

"Only my big pussycat," I replied.

"How did he get up there?"

"Oh you know Reilly. Where there's a will, there's a way. He just got up on the bonnet of your Lada, and from there it was all plain sailing."

"*Sailing?*" exclaimed Kevin, who has a droll sense of humour. "The day I see your cat go off *sailing*, I'll eat my hat."

"Maybe you'd better start eating now," I grinned. "Remember, I told you Reilly's already been swimming with me."

"People should be writing things about *you*, AJ, not the other way round," Shelley remarked.

"Maybe...one day," I conceded, thinking about the few articles which already had been written about me. They were nice little articles, not too in-depth, which was what I wanted. Give 'em the basic facts, I'd decided, and leave out most of the best bits: keep those for an autobiography one day!

Kevin and Shelley left after an hour or so and despite the noises made by the cats, the cottage seemed awfully quiet. I read for a couple of hours; the thought niggling away at me that I really must work on an article for one of the twelve publications I regularly wrote for. The quote "procrastination is the thief of time" is well said, but in my book a little procrastination gives us time for a rest. And rest was something I did not get a lot of, with deadlines to meet every week - and often every day.

**

The next day I was aware that Katie had not come home. I hoped that she wasn't stuck on a roof somewhere, as she had been in the past. I thought about her and thought about other articles I still had to write, but lacked not only the incentive right then, but also the inspiration. For some odd reason, I could not get enthused about writing a couple of articles on dairy effluent disposal.

Delaying the inevitable, I went outside. Katie still hadn't reappeared and Reilly had his nose down, investigating a small beetle which was doing its best to escape the curiosity of my big cat.

"Where's Katie, Reilly?"

"How should *I* know? I'm not her keeper."

"Yes, but you're always bossing her around and telling her what to do. I thought you'd have a fair idea of where she is."

"Just goes to show you don't know *everything* about me!"

"Oh come on, Reilly, you *must* know where she is!"

He turned away from me and began to wash himself. I was pleased to see the little beetle escape to freedom in the long grass at the edge of the lawn.

"Nope. She's entitled to *some* time away by herself. Them's the breaks, woman!"

"Is this the real Reilly saying this?" I bent to feel his forehead and nose. "My poor wee puss - are you sickening for something?"

"There is no need to be sarcastic, woman."

I smiled grimly. "Sarcastic? Was I? Oh come *on*, Reilly! Where's little Katie? You know she panics when she gets stuck anywhere."

"So would *you*, if you were stuck!"

"So...I rest my case!"

Reilly just smirked and turned away again, then seemed to change his mind, and walked nonchalantly inside. I marched outside and stood on the small patio.

"Katie!" I called. "Katie!"

From the vicinity of one of the neighbour's houses I heard Katie's unmistakable, piping meow.

"Katie!" I called again. Reilly ventured back outside and sniffed the air in a bored fashion.

"Really, she's the scattiest cat I have ever known!"

"Have you known many?" I asked, craning my neck to see where Katie was. I suspected she was on one of the neighbour's rooftops again.

3

"One or several," Reilly replied archly, giving himself a cursory wash.

I turned back to him. "You mean you actually let them get that close?"

"I was in a particularly patient mood and they wanted to admire me from close up."

"Bighead!"

"Can I help it if I'm so good-looking?"

"I suppose not," I conceded with a grin.

Katie gave another plaintive meow, this time a lot closer. Yes, she was on the next-door neighbour's roof. I went to the house and knocked on the door and Sheryl, the seemingly-aloof neighbour answered.

"Hi Sheryl. My cat's on the roof again."

"Not that Reilly again?"

"No, Katie this time. She likes to explore then she panics because she can't get back down. At least, she *thinks* she can't."

"Daft, isn't she?"

"Yes, she is a bit."

Sheryl gave a quick smile and added: "there's a ladder there. You'll have to get her down yourself though - I'm off to work."

"Thanks, Sheryl." I turned away as she closed the door and saw the ladder lying against the fence. I propped the ladder up against the wall in the most strategic and safest place I deemed possible and, after five minutes of encouraging Katie, finally I was able to grab her, hold her close and carry her down.

What a relief it was to have her safe. She'd been out all night and was wet and cold.

"Bed for you after a good breakfast, my girl," I said tenderly.

"Huh!" Reilly snorted when I carried Katie inside. "You don't fuss over *me* like that!"

"Yes I do! At least I *would*, but you won't let me!"

"I do when it suits me!"

"You said a mouthful, cat."

Reilly stared at Katie. "Youse get up dere and youse too scared to get down without Mummy's help. You wanna get on in life, kid? Youse do things by yerself! Dem's the breaks!"

"I've heard you say that before," Katie piped. "You have very bad speech, Reilly."

"I'm a tough cat, dat's why. Take what I said before as meant."

"I'll ignore you Reilly. I've had a nasty fright!"

"Silly little girl cat," Reilly sniggered. He moved away from us and found a piece of newspaper to tear to pieces.

I gave Katie a good rub-down with a towel and she purred in great pleasure - half of that I was sure was simply because she was so relieved to be back home again. I'd lost count of the times that Katie had done this sort of thing, and I wondered if she would ever learn.

**

A few days later when I was outside I was aware of movement on top of the other neighbour's steep, A-framed roof. It was Reilly this time, who was on a neighbour's roof. He went right to the apex, sat at the end and looked out over what he deemed to be his territory.

"Look at me, woman! I'm da king of da castle and you're da dirty rascal!"

"Reilly, come on down from there this instant, before you fall!" I hoped my neighbours didn't see him, and even more so, their cat Misty. His nose would really be put out of joint, I thought.

Too late, the euphemistically-named Misty espied Reilly.

"Get off my human's roof!"

"Make me, fat, ginger cat!"

"You are a nasty, grey and white cat. Get off there before I come and get you off, I'm warning you!"

"Youse, and whose army would you use? It would take dat much to shift a pussycat such as me!"

"If you think you're so smart, why do you talk like an alley cat sometimes?"

"Elementary, fat, *alley* cat! So that cats like you can understand!"

"Hiss! Come down!"

"Make me! Make me! You can't, can you? Because youse is too fat and lazy to get up here! Go away, you silly fat, ginger thing."

"Hiss! I'll get you one of these days!"

"Better cats dan youse have tried and failed."

Misty hissed again and walked away. Reilly stretched and washed himself. Even from where I was standing, I could see he had a smug look. Five minutes later he arrived home, chirruping with glee.

"I put dat Misty in his place."

"You are not very neighbourly," I remarked.

"Even *you* have said he's not very nice at times," Reilly reminded me.

I agreed, and watched as he bounded out the back door and frolicked around under the clothesline. Back inside he came, and leaped onto the bench to investigate the sound of water running into the sink.

"I love dat sound. It reminds me of the beach. Can we go to the beach?"

"Not right now, cat. I've got things to do."

"I wanna go to the beach."

"I said no, not right now. What's the matter with your hearing?"

"Nothing, woman. I heard you the first time!"

"Then why don't you take no for an answer?"

"Because I figure it's worth working on you for a while. All you females give in, sooner or later."

"Only when it suits us," I said with a grin, remembering Reilly's "only when it suits me".

"Hah! Dat's what you say *now!* You're changing the subject, woman! I wanna go to the beach!"

"Later, Reilly. I've got housework to do and an article to write."

"Have some fresh air, woman. You'll write far better after you've been out in the fresh air!"

"What would *you* know about it?"

I'd swear he smiled as he watched me stack dishes in the warm, soapy water.

"Haven't I already told you we cats have been around for a very long time? What else is there to learn about life?"

"Have it your way, then, cat."

"And so I shall. I like the look of this water. Here, let me test it." He dipped his paw in and patted at the suds.

Despite myself, I stopped washing the dishes to see what he would do next. He patted the suds with his other paw, looked up at me with a gleam in his great, golden eyes, then casually stepped into the sink on top of the previous night's dinner plates. I laughed.

"Oh Reilly! What a sight you look!"

He lifted each paw in turn and flicked suds at me.

"Ugh! Did you *have* to do that?"

"Of course I did! You wouldn't take me to the beach. So I'm having a paddle in the sink! You can take it or leave it!"

"I'd prefer to leave it. Get out of the sink, cat."

With that, he shook each paw again, plonked his paws back in the warm, soapy water, and then, with a wriggle of his bottom, he leaped onto the bench and soap suds went over me and over the floor. He then proceeded to shake each paw yet again.

It was revenge, I knew. The front of my blouse was by now quite wet and the dishes were taking me several times as long to wash. I let the water out, ran hot water over the plates, and filled the sink again, squeezing in a good dollop of dishwashing liquid. With a scornful look, Reilly gave himself a cursory wash and then, with a triumphant chirrup, leaped onto the floor and enjoyed skidding across the short stretch of vinyl flooring.

"Yah! Seamus O'Reilly...Olympic skater!"

"Olympic bighead," I said with amusement.

"Silly woman, you don't recognize talent when it's right under your nose!"

With that last comment, he chirruped and made a beeline for my bedroom.

**

7

All the same, I took Reilly for a walk to the beach a short while later. As Katie was reluctant about going, it didn't take us long. At least it *shouldn't* have taken us long, but Reilly diverted up and into the big old pine tree on the Carter's Beach Domain.

"Come down from there!" I called. A couple out for a stroll looked amusedly at me. "Reilly!" I called again. "I want to go back home now. Come down!"

"Is that your little boy up the tree?" asked the female half of the couple. She sported that smiling, doting look that very maternal women often wear.

"I guess you could say that," I replied. "It's my cat."

"Oh? Your *cat?*" She gave me a wary look and tucked her arm into her husband's, then steered him away.

"Strange young lady," I heard her say, but I didn't care, as long as my cat came home with me. The scenario reminded me of times in the past when similar incidents happened and the conversation was almost the same.

It had been a short walk so I visited my neighbour Lorraine, whom Katie often visited. On this particular day Reilly came too, having plenty of energy to spare after our brief time out. He decided that if my toilet was good enough to drink from, then so should Lorraine's be good enough. We heard crashing around in Lorraine's smallest room and rushed in to see what Reilly had got up to this time. Pot plants were upended down the loo.

"Too well scrubbed, dis toilet! What's dis blue stuff in here? It looks poisonous! How do you expect a cat to drink from dat when you've stuck poison down there? I feel sorry for the plants that fell down, of their own accord, mind you. It'll turn 'em blue."

His bottom wriggled and looked so amusing from where we stood.

"Get out of there, Reilly," I said, while trying not to smile.

"Call out da environmentalists! Call out the *guards!* You've put poison in the whole system!"

"Don't be silly, Reilly. That's environmentally-friendly stuff for helping keep bugs away."

"Keeping bugs away? *Killing* dem? Call out the guards! Call out the environmentalists! Dis is a war, I say!"

"Fancy saying the plants fell down there of their own accord! Lorraine, there are times when I am so ashamed of my cat," I said sadly, while picking up the dislodged pots of plants and putting them back in place.

Lorraine's smiled wavered a little and I felt even more ashamed.

"Don't worry about it, Amber Jo. Everyone around here knows what he's like," she said.

I heard a distinct sniggering from Reilly.

***

# CHAPTER TWO

## *Discerning Tastes*

Although Katie did not particularly care for shellfish, Reilly had long proved to be a connoisseur of at least several of life's delicacies. He was particularly fond of shellfish as well as whitebait, a tiny fish delicacy nationwide.

I thought of a cat I'd had once, by name of Phoenix. Rising from the ashes? Oh no, just rising via a quick leap to the kitchen bench where frozen whitebait was thawing out. I'd gone out and had forgotten about the thawing whitebait, which had been frozen solid when I left. I was away for a few hours and in the warmth of the afternoon sun pouring through the kitchen window the inevitable happened – the whitebait started thawing out. Phoenix chewed through the plastic wrapper, ate the thawing whitebait and some of the plastic, and promptly vomited everything up onto the kitchen bench. I had returned home and was busy changing out of my "town" clothes in my bedroom. It was the 'whoop whoop' sound that caught my attention. By the time I arrived on the scene, Phoenix had already vanished, leaving the revolting, reeking mess for me to clean up.

It put me off whitebait for some time, I can tell you.

There is something to be said for the adage: the best laid plans of mice and men…etcetera. I'm sure that I'm not the only one who has had to make do with something simple for the evening meal when the cat (or dog) has stolen what was to be the main course.

Another cat I'd had for several years began bringing interesting things home. I thought that maybe Nugget and I could be onto a good thing when he began bringing home fresh beef olives, with barely a tooth mark in them. On another day it was fruit cake, and the following day it was top quality steak. I was surprised that he hadn't chewed them first, since he was partial to all of them and was not averse to stealing fruit cake straight from my hand as I raised it to my mouth.

I gave up on the idea of Nugget and I being in cahoots when he brought home half a rat the following day, and the day after that, a smelly fish head, which he left by the back door in the heat. The smell wafting under the door soon alerted me to its presence, and the swarming, noisy flies added to my alertness.

One day while clearing long grass from the fence down the hill where I lived in Nelson I came across a budgerigar wing. It was then that I realized I hadn't heard the neighbour's budgie chattering away outside in its cage. As the cage was hooked well up from the ground and away from protuberances from where a cat could leap, I still have no idea how Nugget opened the cage and caught the bird. I remember the shame I felt that time, but the neighbours were philosophical about what had happened, even though I could not say categorically that it was *my* cat that had done the awful deed. The neighbours too, were puzzled as to how a cat could reach the cage at the height it was at, and being well away from any paw-hold places that could have given access.

Yes indeed, cats can be thieves - of food, of time, and of neighbors' pets. Some years ago I was told the rather horrible story of some people who had recently bought two miniature Chihuahua puppies, and soon after, had to go away for the weekend. Not wanting to put the valuable and very tiny puppies in kennels, they asked their neighbours if they would care for the puppies. The neighbours agreed, thinking that they weren't doing anything in particular that weekend, and it might be rather fun to look after the tiny pedigree puppies.

But by Sunday afternoon they realized that they had a function they had to attend, one which had temporarily slipped their minds. They decided that the puppies couldn't come to any harm staying inside. They were warm and well fed and sleeping, when the neighbours were ready to leave to attend the function. A couple of hours later when they returned, they went looking for the tiny puppies and the longer they searched, the more anxious they became.

Finally they looked under one of the spare beds - there to find their very fat, very smug cat, with a few bits of puppy hair and skin lying around. Their big cat had eaten well over a thousand dollar's worth of pedigree puppies in one afternoon snack.

I told the story to Reilly, who sniggered happily.

"You are a gross cat," I informed him sternly.

"Really, woman, how naïve of the people to go out and think their big cat is going to look at those runty little things and say: "nice teeny tiny puppies, I will gladly look after you for the afternoon! I will look after you as well as if you were my own babies!" The cat probably thought they were rats. Look how I thought of Inky. I saw him as a big brown rat."

"So you did," I agreed, thinking of Kevin and Shelley's dog Inky - a dear little crossbred with a wonderful nature. "Even so, imagine how the people thought when they realized what had happened!"

"*Thought* being the operative word here, woman! If they'd thought a bit more before they went out, about the possible consequences of leaving a big cat with two tasty morsels, the problem wouldn't have arisen. *And* they would have saved over a thousand dollars!"

"When did you get to be so smart?" I asked waspishly.

"Since the beginning of time," Reilly replied succinctly. "Anyway, what happened in the end? Did the people pay for the expensive snack their cat had eaten?"

"That I don't know."

Reilly sniggered. "I would have suggested to the puppy owners that they could take the cat as exchange. After all, their puppies were inside him!"

"That is really gross."

"I know, but practical, wouldn't you say?"

Off he ran, sniggering again.

**

I did not feel like cooking a meal this particular evening, and as I hadn't bought any takeaway food for quite some time, my conscience was clear. The cats stayed home after their early dinner while I went for a walk to the dairy, which also doubled as a small restaurant and fast food outlet.

The owner was cooking oysters and the smell was delicious. I ordered half a dozen, plus potato chips to take home. Back home, I spread the paper out on the table, fetched the tomato sauce from the cupboard and sat down to enjoy my feast.

"You're having *oysters*? Gimme! Gimme!"

"Only one, Reilly, but don't you dare be sick. These are expensive so I don't want them wasted."

"I have *never* been sick after eating shellfish! Yum yum - oysters for tea." He crunched through the oyster in seconds.

"Oyster, singular, my dear cat. I'm surprised Katie hasn't come out from the bedroom."

"She doesn't like oysters! Can I have her share?"

"No, you greedy cat. You had your dinner before I left."

"We call it tea, here in New Zealand," he reminded me.

"I know, I know...that's left over from the British rule."

He ignored my comment. "Gimme another oyster, woman!"

"No, you can have a chip."

"Potato chip? No thanks! That's human stuff! I am a *cat!*"

"So you keep reminding me, Reilly," I said as I popped another succulent oyster in my mouth and shivered in ecstasy as the large, new season freshly cooked and lightly battered oyster scrunched in my mouth and oyster juices flowed over my tongue. "Mm-mm, that sure is good!"

"You're supposed to *share!*" He glared at me with his great golden eyes and I almost relented.

"You didn't want any chips."

"I didn't want any! What sort of cat do you think I am?"

"Hopefully, one who eats potato chips when offered them. You were a starving cat once, remember."

"I remember it well...but actually, I was still only a defenseless kitten."

"You defenseless? That's a laugh!"

"Laugh away if you must! If that's what makes you happy."

I grinned. "Yes indeed it does. As I was saying, you were a defenseless cat...er, kitten, and when Lou's son Shane found you, you were chewing on a very dead, very dried out old possum. You can't tell me that was tastier than nice, golden, crisp and crunchy potato chips!"

"Dat was then. Dis is now. And I'm still hungry, woman! Gimme another oyster, *now!*"

I sighed. "Okay, if you must, you must. There's no telling *what* you'd do if I continued to refuse you." I'd swear Reilly smiled at that remark, and his next words confirmed it.

"You got *that* in one, woman!" he said smugly. "I'm still having my revenge on humankind for the way I was treated."

"Remember too, Reilly, it was a human who rescued you. And haven't *I* always been good to you?" I said defensively. "Who else would have put up with your bad behaviour for as long as I have?"

"Someone else as daft as you, heh heh. Now, gimme an oyster, before I think of something drastic to do."

Sighing, I handed one to him and he purred as he quickly chomped through it, then stalked over to the sofa to leap onto it. He sat there happily, washing his face.

"Thanks for dat, woman!" He blinked owlishly at me and yawned. "See, I really *am* a grateful cat!"

"Yes, you can be when you want, but must you always call me woman?"

"You *are* one, aren't you?"

"Of *course* I am! But I do have another name. It's Amber Jo."

"Yes, like my wonderful eyes, I know, but meaning the amber part. But we can't have *two* of us in this house. So I'll call you woman when it suits me."

I tried to outstare him, while munching on a potato chip, but my stares didn't work too well. Reilly was far better at it than me.

"Woman!"

"Cat!" I replied.

"Woman! Maybe even Catwoman, heh heh!"

"Cat! Oh...what's the use?" I finished off the last of the chips, checked out the scrunched up pieces of waxed paper to see if any oysters were hiding in the folds - alas they were not - then I screwed up the paper and put it in the garbage bin outside.

When I returned Reilly had curled into a ball on the sofa, opened one eye sleepily, and yawned.

"Now, I want some peace and quiet so I can have a nap."

He gave a sigh and settled down into the sofa even further. From where I was sitting at my nice oval dining table, I was sure I could feel him smiling to himself.

Oh indeed, Reilly had me cat-a-logued very well!

I stood up, placed my hands on my hips and loudly stated: "And that is that, said the cat!"

Reilly opened one eye again. "Fancy that! Oh...do shut up woman, and have a nap of your own!"

"Hmmm," I muttered. "I just might do that!" I figured it was still early enough in the evening for a short nap not to affect a good night's sleep. On the way to my bedroom, I peered into Reilly's face. He was indeed smiling. I could even hear him purring softly - something he didn't do very often, especially since growing into an adult cat.

I went into my bedroom where dear little Katie was sleeping soundly in the middle of my bed, her deep tabby markings a wonderful foil against the soft orange bedspread. When I settled on top of the bed next to her and pulled a crocheted rug over top of us, Katie opened her big green eyes and yawned and purred.

"Hello Mother."

"Hello Katie O'Brien. Oh how nice it is to have a beautiful cat who respects me," I whispered.

Katie's eyes were closing in sleep again. "Oh I *do* respect you and I *do* love you! After all, you saved me from a fate worse than death. I was at the mercy of that dreadful big black tomcat at the lodge and you *saved* me! How could I ever forget that? You would have been *shocked* if you could have heard the rude things that cat said to me..."

"I don't think I would somehow, Katie dear," I said softly, but Katie had already fallen asleep again.

**

Katie increasingly came for walks to the beach with Reilly and me, and how proud I felt! Sure, I was the recipient of many a strange look but pride in my cats more than outweighed the odd stares, shaking of heads and occasional, slightly derogatory comments.

I remember a young man saying to me once: "I can see you as a little widdy-woman, when you're old, Amber, in a little cottage, sitting there in a rocking chair knitting away, and surrounded by cats."

Well now, I am neither old nor am I a "widdy-woman", but the young man is correct on nearly one count! I can't exactly say I am surrounded by cats, but then all cat lovers will know that just one cat can have a way of surrounding you, if he or she has a mind to.

Maybe one day in the future that young man will be right on all counts!

Cats have always been a joy to me: their individual markings, dexterity and grace and great character have drawn me to them from as far back as I can remember.

Having lived on a farm for the first ten years of my life, it was a wonderful way of life in that we could roam on the farm almost anywhere we chose. And often as not, a cat or two came with us.

When I was eight years old my brother Dale gave me a little black kitten; it was the first time I had ever been able to consider that a cat or kitten was actually mine. When our mother, without first asking me gave the kitten, named Blackie, to the district nurse, I felt a sense of disappointment, loss and betrayal that I have never forgotten. The same thing happened when I brought home a puppy. My mother gave him away while I was at school, without first talking to me about him. I do have to admit though, that I had a penchant for bringing stray animals home, or insects, rescuing birds and so on. I have been accused of being a rescuer, but so what? There should be more people around who do the same thing, I always say.

"Oh yeah, you rescue stray people too, I believe," Reilly said.

"I thought you were asleep?"

"Your thoughts encroached into my mind and you woke me up. Now give me some peace." He yawned and went back to sleep.

Huh, I thought. What a cheek!

Over the years there have been many cats, some who have just stayed a day or a week or two - just to recharge their batteries on life's path, and have then gone again, presumably on their way home. Each time a gap has been left, but refilled - at least temporarily, by the arrival of another kitten or cat. I have always believed that I was honoured by visits from cats, and I have no doubts whatsoever that these pussycats didn't just stop by for rest and recreation, but were sent by a Higher Source. How else could I explain the fact that they arrived at a time when I was feeling lonely?

God so often works in mysterious ways!

I look back to more recent times, when I had prayed fervently for God to send me a tough tomcat, to keep the dogs from leaving their unpleasant deposits on my lawn. My prayers were answered, although not quite in the way that I had envisaged. It was only after I'd had Reilly for a short while that I thought back to those fervent prayers and realised that God had not only answered my prayers, but had answered them tenfold.

I'm sure He was smiling broadly when He answered them.

And here I was, back at Carter's Beach, albeit not at the same address when Reilly first came to live with me, but only a short walk away. It was so nice to have the long-promised cups of tea with my friend Eileen, whom I'd previously lived next door to, and whom I'd come to know via Reilly's intervention.

When I come to think of it, I often came to know people through Reilly's intervention.

But this time back in Carter's Beach I had wee Katie as well. I think she helped to soften Reilly a bit, and to help support *me* when Reilly was at his most chauvinistic! My friends were amazed at how loving she was...and is, and they wondered how I could have two cats so opposite in nature.

"Imagine if I'd had *two* Reillys?"

"You'd be run out of town," one of my friends was quick to reply.

"Thanks for your vote of support," I replied, slightly aggrieved.

However, I was very much aware that Reilly had already earned himself a reputation and some of my friends didn't visit as often, so maybe my friend's comment was justified.

\*\*\*

# CHAPTER THREE

## *Pussycat Advice*

It was a gorgeous Sunday afternoon with only a few soft clouds in the sky and there was peace all around. Even Reilly was in a mellow mood. I had been to a church service and now I had a delicious afternoon in which I didn't have to catch up on any work for the various publications I wrote for, and so a leisurely walk down the beach was in order.

"Want to come to the beach, pussycats?"

"Of course!"

"Oo, yes please Mum!"

I opened the French door and Reilly raced outside and disappeared over the fence. Katie sauntered outside and sat on the edge of the lawn to wash herself.

I called Reilly home but he didn't immediately return. The phone rang; it was my amusing friend Hubie. I told him I was expecting my cat back home.

"Expecting? You're not *expecting*, are you? To whom?"

I laughed. "I'm expecting Reilly..." I began.

"Good Lord!" he interrupted. "Now the girl tells me she's expecting and the father's a tomcat."

"Hubie, you are a naughty man! I'm expecting Reilly to come back inside. I've been calling for him."

"Oh *now* the girl tells me! You had me worried for a minute!"

"I think it would take a lot to worry *you*, my friend."

"That's right! My advice to you is to keep your pussycats under better control. Let them know who's boss in your house."

"Reilly thinks *he* is," I replied.

"That's what I mean! Cats can be so ungrateful..."

"Not Katie though." It was my turn to interrupt.

"Well, most of them. Now, what you need is a good dog."

"I've already got two cats and anyway, Reilly would attack a dog."

"That doesn't seem right to me. It should be the other way round."

"Believe me, it's not. Not in Reilly's book, anyway. Dogs are there for him to chase and generally give a hard time."

"Well just you take my advice and let them know who's boss."

"Yes Hubie," I said in a long-suffering tone. He laughed and soon afterwards began singing a song about a pretty kitten coming out to play. His voice boomed over the phone and then he rang off. What a character of a man, I thought, and not for the first time, I might add. My ears rang for several minutes afterwards, from the effects of his booming voice. He could have been placed on the bow of a ship and acted as the ship's foghorn, I thought. Pity help the crew on any water craft foolish enough to get too close on a foggy night.

Reilly returned, and stared through the French door in his "Kilroy wuz here" manner. It was one of his ways to get me to open the door without him having to open his mouth. It worked every time.

"Where have you been? Katie and I have been waiting to go to the beach." My ears were still ringing from Hubie's voice.

He stalked inside and leaped onto the sofa. "Just a little matter I had to attend to wiv a dude," he said disdainfully.

"I hope you haven't been having bad words with anyone."

He blinked several times. I knew that meant he was about to - if not tell an outright lie, at least hedge somewhat.

"Who *moi?* Would dis cat have bad words wid anyone?"

"Too right you would! I can always tell...your language deteriorates."

"Huh! Fancy saying such a thing to a cat such as me!"

"Yes, fancy. Now pussycats, do you or do you not want to go to the beach?"

"Oo yes please, Mum!" said Katie, in the same way she had a short while before.

Reilly began washing himself. "I might, if I've a mind to."

"If it wasn't for Katie wanting to go, I've a good mind to stay home!"

Reilly gazed at me innocently. "Hurry up then woman, and let's get on with it! What are you waiting for? We haven't got all day!"

We exchanged glares then, with one bound, Reilly was off the sofa and purring around my legs.

"You know, for a woman, and a human one at that, *and* a short one, you ain't half bad."

"Oo Reilly, you can be *so* sweet to Mum!"

He snickered as we left the cottage.

"I know. I consider that a weakness!"

As almost always, he had the last word.

**

I thought back to some of the other cats I'd had in the past; one was named Muffy and I'd had her for many years. Her original name was 'Wee Amber', named by her then owner, my friend Eve. It was disconcerting when visiting Eve to hear her say: "here Amber, come on Wee Amber, there's a good girl." One day when I was visiting Eve and was in a silly mood I got down on my hands and knees and crawled over to Eve, giving a very good rendition of meowing and purring.

"What a woman! Oh boy!" She rolled her big blue eyes heavenwards and said to no-one in particular: "she sure is *different!*"

Eve had asked me if I would like to have the little tortoiseshell cat, as she already had several cats of her own, plus an assortment

21

of dogs. As it happened, this "different" little woman one day took Wee Amber home, and re-named her Muffy. Just because she looked like a Muffy. Eve had named her Wee Amber because of the ginger in her tortoiseshell colouring. She reminded her of me, Eve said. I wasn't sure how to take that. Some years later I thought back to what Eve had said when, one day while still living in Nelson my young son Vinnie said to me: "say Mum, you know how Muffy is...kind of short and small..."

"Yes my son?" I prompted warily.

"Well, you know how she's kind of ginger and mottled?"

"Y-esss?" My eyes narrowed.

"And you know how she's sort of funny and daft?"

"Y-esss?" I said again, my voice lowered. "What are you trying to tell me?"

"Gee she reminds me of you!"

"Thank you my dear little son! Very charming, I must say. Somehow I knew you were going to come out with something like that."

Vinnie just grinned, his big blue eyes twinkling merrily.

"Little, ginger and daft I can cope with, but I'm not so sure about the mottled bit," I said edgily.

"That's because your hair is in different shades of gold," Vinnie replied. I stared at him. This time he was serious, and I accepted what he said as a compliment.

Muffy had often amused us with her daft ways; one of them was when she would "catch" a piece of meat from her bowl, when yowling and chattering, and would bring it to me to show me just what a clever cat she had been. The same applied to when she would bring in a worm or two, or a grass grub. I would still tell her what a clever little cat she had been and she would purr noisily in gratitude for my praise.

**

Of all the cats I've had over the years, they have all been wonderfully unique; some gentle, some sweetly daft, some very tough like Honeybelle of Mandalay whom I mentioned in a previous story, and some other cats who were ships in the night. Or should I say cats in the night - whimsical little things which came to me for bed and lodgings for a night or several and left a gap in my heart when they moved on.

But of all those pussycats that brought such pleasure (and pain) over the years, none has equaled Reilly, that dreadful, adorable cat.

"Writing about me again, were you?"

I jumped in surprise. "Blimey, where did *you* spring from?"

He narrowed his eyes at me as I was writing this and came to sit on the table, to stare down at my rough draft written in longhand.

"I am the dark phantom of the night..."

"But it's still daytime."

"The dark phantom who goeth wherevereth he's needed..."

"Whither thou goest, cat - you can goest off this table and stop poking at my pen!"

"Must you spoil a good story?" He lowered his head, his great golden eyes gleaming with mischief. "The moving finger writes, and having writ, moves on!"

He took a swipe and knocked the pen flying from my hand.

"Reilly!"

"Woman! What speed I possess! What masterful cunning! The moving pen really has moved on!"

"What an ego!" I retorted, retrieving my pen and rubbing my fingers where his claws had caught me, leaving a fine red trail of blood. "You scratched me, you awful cat."

"I don't care. I get bored when you're not taking any notice of me."

"As I said before, what an ego. And get off the table."

He ignored me. "I think I'll go and pick on Katie."

"You leave her alone! She's sleeping and doesn't want to be disturbed."

"She's a sooky cat, but I'll say one thing for her."

"And what's that?"

Reilly looked smug as he sat there, still on the table.

"She thinks I'm handsome, which I am, of course! She's got such good taste!"

**

My father told me once about our cousin Diane's Siamese cat, named Garçon, who proved to be better than almost any guard dog. He carried his protectiveness to great lengths unfortunately, or fortunately, depending on which way you looked at it. Any person who came to the door was deemed to be a stranger and therefore of a deeply suspicious character. Garçon would hide just around the corner and when the door was answered by my uncle or one of the other family members, Garçon would spring around the corner and leap up, sinking claws and fangs into the hapless visitor.

Many were the people who stumbled back down the footpath, bleeding and in shock. Dad, who also had a great affection for cats, had no sympathy for the people at all.

"Cats are smart, and Garçon was one of the smartest cats I knew," he said. "A lot of those visitors were religious cranks. Garçon soon sorted them out! They never came back again."

There are numerous other tales I could tell about cats I have personally known or have heard interesting stories about, but most of those will have to wait for another time. Indeed, cats of all markings and sizes have come and gone in my life. It seemed to me that as far back as I could remember, there had been a cat to cuddle and talk to.

When I had returned to the West Coast after spending nearly a year in Australia, I had moved into a small apartment where the landlady, who lived in the adjoining apartment, stipulated "no pets". Normally I would have turned down the offer, but as rental properties were in short supply when I returned I had no alternative but to accept what was available. Being cat-less, I had to make the most of her cat Lockie, short for her owner's maiden name of Lockington. Lockie is a blue Persian with not very nice manners.

Still, as far as I was concerned, a cat is a cat and should he or she want to visit me, then I felt privileged. Sometimes it rankled though, when Lockie would meow outside the window of my tiny lounge area, and I would be expected to open the window and let her in. As soon as she'd had a drink of milk and maybe a small snack, off she'd go again, the fur around her mouth white with milk deposits.

With her grumpy face, the addition of a milk moustache gave her a comical look and I often laughed. She'd glare at me, lick her whiskers then demand to be let outside.

My friend Hubie had given me a trick Santa Claus bag. It was really a small red satin rectangular cushion with a big Santa Claus face covering the front of it. When you squeezed it a piercing 'Ho ho ho! Aha, aha aha!' would issue forth. I was tidying up the lounge area on one particular day and popped the lightly padded bag behind a cushion in an armchair. I promptly forgot about it as I went about my other chores.

A little later in the day I was just outside the only door into my apartment when Lockie wanted to come inside. I let her in and gave her a small snack, as was the usual pattern. Soon afterwards she wanted to go back outside and as I leaned my knee on the cushion to reach forward to open the window, a resounding 'ho ho ho! Aha, aha, aha!' pierced forth and Lockie flew up in the air. I almost did too. Lockie clawed at the window to be let outside, and as I leaned forward again to open the window for her, I leaned against the hidden Santa Claus cushion again and the 'ho ho ho! Aha, aha, aha!' promptly began again. It took a while for my heart to stop racing.

Many weeks passed by before Lockie returned to visit.

In some ways she is reminiscent of Reilly, although at that stage Reilly was not even a twinkle in a tomcat's eyes. It was in her demanding ways and the frequent glares if she couldn't get her own way. As I still remember her fondly, I referred to her as Miss Charlotte Lockington, because that seemed to suit her far better than simply Lockie.

## *Sweet Charlotte Lockington*

Rain cloud coloured
and soft as mist
with wild amber eyes
and fearsome scowl.

Dainty mouth opened forth
in a plaintive meow
tufted ears flickering
alert - always alert

and ready for the sound
of the refrigerator door.
Miss Charlotte Lockington
and I hold forth
on conversations that go like this:

*Sweet Charlotte Lockington,*
*must you only visit me*
*on your own demands?*
*Saucer of milk?*
*What about a cuddle first?*

Oh cunning, cunning soft and sweet
Miss Charlotte Lockington
takes her milk so daintily;
looks at me with
her wild amber eyes
and glares, yes glares
at my inhospitality.

*If I can't have cream*
*I may as well leave*
I suppose she's thinking.

Off she goes with a soft misty leap
out the window
via the way she came,
no thanks forthcoming
nor a grateful look
as she stalks away:
*I think she's already forgotten me.*

**

The poem was published in a fairly large volume of my poetry. I wrote the poem before the incident with the Santa Claus bag/ cushion, and I think it is now reasonable to assume Lockie has *not* forgotten me!

I think of her often, when I think of Reilly. Maybe it's also the association with the amber eyes and the frequent glares; at least some of the other colouring, and long fur that causes me to link the two. I was in that small apartment which was haunted (and perhaps that's the real reason for Lockie not staying long!) for just over two years before I moved to Martin Place in Carter's Beach, where soon after I was to meet Reilly for the first time.

**

The day I moved to Carter's Beach, just one day before St Patrick's Day, was a dismal one with teeming rain. I clearly remember trudging out to my red and deep charcoal grey Mazda sports car in my little red gumboots and raincoat. I briefly wondered at how many people could say that their gumboots matched the colour of their sports car, but that brief thought failed to cheer me.

I hunched over the carton in my arms to keep as much rain off as possible, and had no alternative but to stand in a big puddle to lift the carton into the back of the Mazda. It was a RX7 model with a hatch door. Unfortunately the hydraulics on the hatch door weren't working properly and just as I bent over to place the carton of goods in my car, the hatch came down with a thump onto the back of my head.

Needless to say I let out a loud "ouch!" and extricated myself and as I did so the chilly rain ran down inside my raincoat. *Things can only get better,* I thought - but I was not to know about Reilly until a short while later that year.

As I write this, I see Reilly on the high fence between my rented townhouse and the old house next door. I looked up because I heard a plaintive meow and any cat lover will relate to the feelings I have whenever I hear a distinctively plaintive meow.

No, it wasn't Reilly, but another cat - Gemma, who lived next door and wanted to go inside. She's definitely a cat who likes home comforts. Reilly gave only a cursory glance around at her meows; he was too busy staring into the kitchen window next door - no doubt disconcerting them to the degree they'll either close their curtains or throw a snack to him.

It's probably both.

\*\*\*

# CHAPTER FOUR

## *Testing The Waters*

I remember back to an amusing incident at Martin Place. As happened frequently on the West Coast of the South Island, we had torrential rain which was too much for the stormwater drains to cope with and the overflow often formed a lake which spread part way across the street. On this particular day the sun had come out again and everything had that wonderfully fresh look and scent.

There wasn't even a breeze and the air was exquisite. Reilly was more than ready to get out and explore. First on his list of things to explore was the pool of water on the street out the front. I went out quietly to observe him...why? Simply because Reilly is such an interesting cat, that whenever he looks intent on exploring or doing something different, you can almost guarantee that it will be highly entertaining.

He was literally "testing the waters". He patted the water on one side, and then he walked around the end of the small lake to the middle of the street, to sit there and pat the water on that side. He began to paddle at the edges then stepped out and shook his paws, giving each a very brief lick.

He appeared to have lost interest altogether - by walking casually to the other side of the street - but then he suddenly turned and galloped towards the deepest section of the water and plunged in, to happily swim around for a moment or two before getting out and shaking himself.

I laughed heartily. "Really cat, you are the limit! I suppose you think you can come in and drape your wet self over my furniture now?"

He yawned then started washing himself, ignoring me.

"You could have gone for a swim at the beach," I said, encouraging him.

"Maybe, but I wasn't in the mood for all that wild surf down there at the beach after the rain. Besides, this is nice and handy. Oh I *did* enjoy that!"

He gazed at me for a few seconds and yawned again, his fangs glinting in the sunlight streaming through the ranch slider door; his mouth showed wonderfully pink.

"Worn out already?" I said with amusement.

"Certainly not! But you should know we cats need to cat-nap. I think I'll have a lie-down, preferably on the sofa."

"Not while you're wet, you're not!" I said firmly.

"Then dry me off, woman, dry me!"

"What did your last slave die of? Overwork?" I said waspishly.

Reilly's eyes narrowed. "Think, woman, *think!* We were sacred in Egypt! Of *course* our slaves died of overwork! You just got lucky; a few thousand years later I hardly work you at all!"

"That's big of you. I'm so grateful," I said dryly.

"So you should be!"

With that parting shot he shook himself once more, ran past me up the steps into the house, and flung himself onto the sofa, falling asleep almost immediately.

Ruefully I noticed the damp spots spreading out from where he was lying. I fetched a towel and Reilly opened one eye on my return.

"Good girl. Now give me a gentle drying off and then leave me in peace."

I muttered under my breath and wondered for the umpteenth time why I put up with such a chauvinistic cat.

"That's because you love me!"

"I never said anything!"

He opened an eye. "I heard your thoughts."

"You are too clever by far," I mumbled.

"We cats are all-seeing, all powerful..."

He closed the eye and soon I felt his deep rumble of purring while asleep.

**

I have always felt we should be careful of what we pray for - that what we want is also what God wants for us.

A few years ago when I fervently prayed for a tough tomcat to alleviate the problem of numerous and regular "doggie-doos" on my lawn, God answered my prayer in an amazing way. He did not send me a tough tomcat...but even better, He sent me Reilly, a very tough tom*kitten*, and my life has never been the same since. God in His wisdom, also knew there would be occasions when I, as a young, single woman would be subject to unwanted advances from the odd male or two.

Maybe "odd" was the operative word in this case.

Reilly had come to stay with me only weeks before and despite his hyperactivity, there were several of these occasions in which I was very glad of his presence. Due to a now-resolved medical problem I was often subject to the miseries of influenza. On this particular occasion when I was recovering from 'flu, it was the scheduled evening for our Poetry Society evening, to be held at my home.

I asked my friend Jan if she would mind staying behind after the meeting as there was someone coming whom I felt uneasy about.

We will call the person Bertie, to protect anonymity.

"Is it Bertie?" Jan asked.

"Yes," I replied. "How did you guess?"

"I had a feeling you didn't care for him."

She agreed to stay behind and out-sit Bertie. The evening was very successful, with a great deal of laughter, poetry reading, and a delicious supper afterwards.

The evening wore on: everyone left except Jan and Bertie. I was exhausted, but lasting better than I expected under the circumstances. By one o'clock in the morning, Jan, who had been suppressing yawns for the past half hour said she had to leave; that she was really tired after her long day at her job as a hearing tutor. I stood up and said I was really tired too, that I was ready for bed and had a big day coming up the next day.

I hoped that Bertie would take the hint when Jan left, but he hung around. I yawned pointedly, and reiterated that I really was tired. I quietly sent up a little prayer of concern as it was obvious that Bertie was going to make a play for me. Just as Bertie tried to put an arm around me and I neatly stepped to one side, Reilly, who was sleeping in his room, woke up and made a terrible din of meowing as loud as his little body would allow, and scratched vigorously at the door.

"Oh, that *kitten!*" Bertie exclaimed, annoyed at the interruption. But I was pleased at the prompt response to my silent, quick prayer.

"He wants to come out - he's had his sleep." *Thanks, God!* I added quietly. I hid a smile when Bertie went to Reilly's room to let him out.

"Oh *pooh!* What a stench! Ooooh!"

Reilly had been to the toilet in his litter box. I declare God has a great sense of humour: I don't think I have ever smelt such *bad* kitten feces! But in this situation they were ideal for my rescue. Bertie made an enormous fuss about the smell and to be sure it was bad, but I still grinned as I entered the spare bedroom where small, feisty Reilly usually slept, and opened the window.

Bertie was still making a fuss about the smell; moaning and complaining bitterly. I was doing my best not to smile.

"Fair go, Bertie! What a lot of fuss about a bad smell. I'll get the air freshener." I fetched an environmentally-friendly container of Rawleigh's boronia-scented air freshener and liberally sprayed it around the room and down the narrow hall, while smiling with grim amusement.

"*Pooh!* That's just about as *bad!* Ooooh, my poor sinuses!"

"For goodness' sake!" I exclaimed. "This stuff smells *gorgeous*, and anyway, it was *you* who sold it to me. You *said* it was environmentally-friendly!" I held out the can and showed it to him, pointing at the wording on the label. "See here Bertle, it says it's safe for the environment!"

"Huh, well it's played havoc with my sinuses. I'm going home. I feel dreadful!" He snuffled and snorted and Reilly left his room with a smug look. I removed the litter box and took it outside, via the back ranchslider, to clean it out after Bertie had gone outside, and quickly re-entered the house. Bertie donned his cycle gear and headed off, sniffing and sneezing. I felt such a rapport with little Reilly as he sat neatly on the steps next to me.

We watched Bertie until he was out of sight. I thought amusedly, *on yer bike, mate!*

"Thanks Reilly. You sure saved me from some unpleasantness."

"I ain't just a pretty face y'know."

"I can see *that!* Did you realise that God sent you to me?"

"Yeah, of *course* I knew that. I hope you're grateful."

"Oh I am!" I said happily, as I picked him up and cuddled him. "Reilly, already you're proving to be a friend in need!"

His crackling purr rattled and rumbled against my face as I'd held him to me and had stroked his vibrant fur.

"Yeah well, just don't get too cosy, huh? I gotta keep up my tough image."

"What, at *your* tender age?"

"An early start sets us cats up for life, woman."

"*Woman?* Good heavens kitty, you sound like a world-weary man!"

"Hey babe, I've got thousands of years of experience behind me...and don't you forget it!"

"I'll try not to, your majesty," I'd said, amused.

"Glad to hear you're showing a little respect."

After Bertie would have been well away up the road, I went back outside to clean out the litter box. Reilly came with me, chattering. "Didn't I save it up well? Huh, huh?"

"You sure did, Reilly!" I laughed.

I was so grateful to my little kitten. I had not wanted to spoil the final part of the evening by getting angry with Bertie, but I would have if necessary.

Instead, my quick prayer was answered, and in the best way possible!

**

That was just one of several occasions in which Reilly saved me from an awkward situation. About eighteen months later when I had spent six and a half months in Motueka before returning to Carter's Beach, another incident occurred in which I was particularly grateful for Reilly's presence.

I was returning from posting away articles and getting other chores done in the township - just a couple of weeks or so after my return south to the West Coast, when I noticed a detour sign had been erected at the entrance to the street on which I usually traveled down to reach my home. The man there, whom I shall call Robert, told me I couldn't go down that street as there was a "detour" sign up.

"Yes," I said, smiling. "I had noticed. Anyway, I'll go the other way home."

"You'll have to go around the other way. We're putting in new sewerage pipes."

"I know that. Anyway Robert, how are you? I haven't seen you for a long time."

"Good, good, but you'll have to go the other way, there's a detour sign up."

"Yes Robert, I can see that," I replied patiently. "I know I'll have to go the other way."

"Do you remember that time you and I had dinner together?"

"You and I? When was that? Surely I couldn't forget something like that!" My mirth was increasing...maybe it was something to do with the fact that I had completed my assignments and had them sent away on time and the sense of relief was making me particularly light-hearted.

"It was when I was working as a bus driver...you remember, we went to Seddonville."

I laughed. "Yes Robert, now I remember. But there were ten others of us there, you drove the bus and that was several years ago!"

He dismissed these facts as if they were of no consequence.

I had been invited, along with all the staff of the bus company, to a farewell dinner for a staff member who was leaving to travel south. I was invited because I was the editor of that branch of a Coast-wide newspaper, and the office I used was leased from the bus company. I also believe my invitation was strengthened by the fact that we brought business to the bus company.

"I wanted to make love to you that night!"

My stomach muscles knotted in amusement.

"Really?" was all I could think of replying, without bursting into laughter.

"But I decided I wouldn't," he said bluntly.

"You mean I had no say in the matter?" I asked, grinning broadly.

"Yeah well, I thought I'd better not on the first date!"

"How very considerate of you! Especially as I didn't know we were technically on a date. Maybe we actually were, along with all the other ten people," I said, my voice quaking. "That's a big date to go on! Well then, I must be off!"

"Yeah, but you can't go this way...there's a detour sign up!"

"Thank you for telling me!" And off I went, laughing heartily.

My former neighbour Eileen visited soon after I arrived home and we had a good laugh about the incident.

About half an hour after she'd left I was preparing vegetables when there was a knock at the door. *Rats!* I thought, when I turned to see a man at the French doors, already taking off his gumboots. *Foiled!* I thought at first that it was a farmer whom I knew, who had seen my little red sports car in the carport. He was a man whom I took pains to avoid because although he was well into retiring age, he made no secret of the fact he liked women and his hands were likely to stray. He especially liked visiting *single* women, and I was one of those on his list. My friend Wendy and I used to give each other a call, depending on whom the farmer visited first. Wendy, who was single like me was also subject to unexpected visits from the farmer, and we would call each other up just after the farmer had left, to warn the other. Sometimes we had enough time to be officially "out" (read that as hiding!), but other times not.

"Come in," I said in a resigned tone, mentally adding I was going to point out I was busy as I was going out soon, which was true. When I turned to see who was there, it wasn't the farmer at all, but Robert.

"You remember what I said earlier about making love to you?" he said, the pointed look he gave me reminding me of a fox.

"I remember well," I said as I turned back to finish peeling potatoes and to hide my returning mirth.

"I meant it! Ooooh, that's what I like about you...your nice little rear!" He quickly dashed over to the sink where he grabbed at my "little rear".

"Clear off!" I said smartly, slapping him. "You can go home right now, Robert, or you can sit down and behave yourself!"

He promptly sat at the table, unabashed. Although I should add here, slapped, but not bashed! "Have you got a boyfriend?" When I said a very prompt "yes", he wanted to know who my boyfriend was. I told him it was Keith, who was known to Robert. "Oh what a shame!" Robert added. I mentally resolved to tell Keith at the earliest opportunity he was my boyfriend, at least temporarily!

"I always fancied you...you know...*ow!*"

"Ow?" I reiterated. "It would be "ow" all right, if I did to you what the average woman would do after being told the things you told me! Lucky for you I don't own a rolling pin."

"Ow! Ow!" Robert was bending down and for a start I couldn't see what was wrong. Then I saw it. "It" was Reilly, who had sunk his claws and teeth into Robert's leg.

"Dat'll teach you for messing wid my human!"

"Get this ferocious cat *off* me!" Robert yelped.

"Oh dear, are you offended? But Reilly's in a *good* mood! You should see him when he's in a *bad* mood!"

"You shouldn't have such a dangerous animal here!"

"What, my handsome cat Reilly *dangerous*? You must be mad!" Inwardly I was quaking with mirth, and doing my best not to let laughter escape.

"I've a good mind to report your cat to the authorities."

"Oh my my, and what a good story I would have to tell *them*..." I said meaningfully.

"I'm leaving...*ow!*"

Reilly had made another attack. "Take dis memory wid you for good measure!"

"Goodbye, Robert," I said, allowing myself to smile broadly as he limped to the door and went outside to put his gumboots back on before leaving.

"Reilly, you must have bitten him awfully hard!" I said to my now big cat, who was sitting by the door, glaring at Robert and swishing his tail.

"Not hard enough, woman. Want me to have another go?"

"Save your biting power, pussycat. Robert's leaving."

"You probably *taught* him to do that," Robert said, as he headed towards his car. "You're *dangerous*, like your cat!"

I stood there next to my cat and folded my arms. "Just as long as you remember that, Robert."

"The funny thing is...you don't look dangerous...you look, oh I don't know, all soft and feminine..." He broke off when he saw Reilly getting ready to spring, eyes glinting dangerously and tail swishing madly.

"I think you'd better get going while you're still in one piece," I advised Robert.

He leaped into his car and just before he backed down my drive he said: "Oh by the way, you can't go down Golf Links Road. You'll have to make a detour."

"I'll remember that," I said with a grim smile.

He roared away and I heaved a sigh of relief. I hoped he'd forget his own advice, drive down Golf Links Road and land in the deep trench prepared for the laying of the new sewer pipes. And preferably if there was old sewage that had leached out of the old pipes and was sitting in the bottom of the trench.

"Really, woman, dat man was mad! You can't do without me, can you?" Reilly remarked.

"I suppose not."

"What would you have done if he had got a bit heavier with you?"

I knew what he was getting at.

"Punched him on the nose," I replied.

Reilly sat to wash himself in his wonderfully nonchalant manner. "I think my way was best. You can be too polite to people like dat you know, and it doesn't get you very far. Dis way, you avoided having to punch dat man on the nose."

"There speaks the voice of great wisdom," I replied and carried on with preparing my evening meal. "However, I didn't think that punching someone on the nose was considered being too nice."

"Yeah, but I meant dat it shouldn't even get to dat stage. I hope you're grateful for my efforts."

"I sure am, pussycat! Here, come to Mum!" I scooped him up for a cuddle.

"Ergh! Gerroff!"

Katie entered the room and blinked owlishly. "What's been happening while I've been asleep?"

Reilly steered her back into the bedroom. "Let me just tell you everything Katie..." I heard him saying as they left the room.

The next day my friend Keith visited. "I hope you don't mind, Keith, but I sort of borrowed you for a boyfriend, in name, at least."

"I don't mind at all."

I told him what had happened the previous afternoon.

"Yeah, but he's as thick as three short planks anyway!"

"I don't know how to take that!" I defended. "Do you mean he's as thick as three short planks because he tried to get fresh with me, or because he's that way, anyway?"

"Both!" Keith replied with a huge grin. I threatened to hit him for being so cheeky. "See what I mean? Anyone who would try to take you on should have their heads read!"

"Thanks very much!" I said defensively. "Nice to know I have such good friends!"

"I was only kidding you. I still mean it though. He wouldn't have got very far before you donged him on the head."

Mollified, I reviewed the scene. "Anyway, Reilly helped me out as well."

"Word will soon get around that you're not to be messed with."

"Yes, I have my built in bodyguard!" I said smugly, and looked down at Reilly, whose eyes were gleaming with mischief.

"A formidable pair, you two," Keith remarked with a grin. "Even *I* would think twice about getting smart with you!"

"I'm glad about that, Keith. Look at Reilly - he's already looking at you suspiciously."

"That's why I said I'd think twice about getting smart with you."

"And that's why you and I are still friends," I replied succinctly.

∗∗∗

# CHAPTER FIVE

## *Energy Unlimited*

It was one of those days when, from early on in the morning Reilly got into mischief. He started the day by clawing his way around the side of my mattress base, the "thwock thwock" sounds highly irritating in the still, clear morning air. When I yelled at him he chirruped and leaped onto my duchess, skidded on the crocheted doilies and sent bottles of lotions and potions flying.

Instead of being frightened by the sound of the clattering bottles, he seemed delighted by it.

"Hey, look at me! I love to skid! Look at the mess I can make in just a few seconds! Listen to the noise I can create with all these bottles of this and that!"

"Get off, get *off,* Reilly!" I yelled.

"Okay woman!" He chirruped, then leaped down from the duchess and resumed clawing his way around my mattress base, pulling threads as he went. I lunged at him, but all he did was chirrup again and squeeze under the base, his fluffy bottom looking hilarious as he wriggled underneath. I tapped his bottom firmly and told him what a naughty cat he was, and out shot a paw, claws extended, and missed my hand by a fraction.

"Get your hands off my rear!" he growled, but I was sure I heard a snigger behind the growl. He turned over on his back and clawed his way across the scrim-type backing under the base and shot out the other side. Katie, who was sleeping on one of the pillows, opened her big green eyes, yawned and went back to sleep.

Reilly had slept well - his energy levels were a pretty good indication of that! Up onto the kitchen bench he leaped, knocking a coffee mug into the sink. Fortunately, the coffee mug didn't break. Reilly was silent for a few seconds and, ultra curious as to what mischief he might now be up to, I got out of bed and tiptoed into the open-plan kitchen/dining area. Reilly was standing in the sink, having a drink of water from a dessert plate which had been soaking overnight.

"Hey there, I quite like a bit of custard with my water!"

"Get out of there, Reilly! It's unhygienic!"

"You said it, woman! Good heavens! Now that you've said it, I could have contracted any *number* of diseases from that water! Arrrgh!"

"You cheeky cat!" I took a swipe at him but he ducked, and flung out a paw at me, his claws raking down my hand. I still wear a scar from that incident. *"Ow!"*

Getting him in a firm grip I put him on the floor and he sped away towards the drapes.

"Killjoy! You'd do anything to spoil a pussycat's fun!"

He stopped short, stared hard at the drapes and crouched down, his bottom up in the air a little - and wriggling. I suddenly realized what he was up to.

"*No* Reilly, don't!"

Too late, Reilly launched himself at the upper part of one of the drapes, but his large size was against him. His weight and force brought the full-length drapes plus the rail they were on, crashing to the floor.

Reilly moved around under one gold-orange drape, the hilarious sight of the large moving lump trying to find his way out restored my humour just a little. Then he emerged and blinked owlishly.

"How dare you throw these drapes over me, woman!"

"Don't be silly, Reilly. I know what you're doing - playing pass the guilt on - and it's not going to work!"

"Oh, but I am now a poor, bewildered cat. Just look at me! All I was trying to do was have a bit of fun...life's just not fair at times, is it?"

He looked so bewildered I began to feel sorry for him. "Never mind Reilly," I found myself saying as I fetched my stool to stand on so I could put the drapes back up where they belonged. I stepped down and picked up Reilly who was wonderfully pliant and sank deliciously into my shoulder and rubbed his face against my cheek.

"Y'know, you're not too bad, for a human!"

"Oh Reilly, you're so cute," I said lovingly, beginning to croon to him. But when I heard him snigger I realized that I'd "been had" yet again.

**

My English penpal, whom I shall call Danny, came for a week-long visit with me. I had driven across the island the day before, staying with my sister Sandy and her family overnight and I met with Danny at the Christchurch International Airport the following morning. Some of his family members, already living in Christchurch, were also there to meet him. Born in New Zealand of an Irish father and English mother, when he was just a young child the family returned to England. Some years later Danny's father passed away.

Danny had always wanted to return to New Zealand, to see the land of his birth. His Cockney accent is very strong and he has the great humour of the Irish and Cockney combined. So it was an entertaining trip back to the Coast, to my small cottage. I'd spent days getting everything ready, including borrowing a trailer and collecting a spare bed of mine which had been kept in storage for some time out at Cape Foulwind.

Being stored in a garage right at the sea edge, the metal parts of the bed had surface rust, but a good rub-down with a bit of sandpaper, finished with another rub-down, this time using a rag soaked in sewing machine oil soon had the rust removed.

Since Danny is quite a big fellow I gave him my bed and set up the single bed in my office, after rearranging the furniture. It was quite a squeeze but I managed, and when Danny arrived he was very grateful for a nice big bed to sleep in. As he was still jet-lagged, he slept on and off the next day. On the following day I showed him the scenery around the district, much to his pleasure.

Reilly and Katie liked him; he was very kindly towards them and was amused by their names. Katie positively *flirted* with Danny, while Reilly looked on in amused tolerance.

"*I* don't have to try to get attention, but look at *you,* you silly little cat! Anyone would think the human was your long-lost soul-mate!"

"You're a jealous, beastly cat, Reilly, so there! This human *likes* me...why *shouldn't* I make up to him?"

Reilly appeared to shrug, and turned his face away in a sudden, aloof manner. "Couldn't care less *what* you do...even if I do think you're a bit fickle!"

"Oh Reilly, are you really jealous? Does that mean you love me?"

He gave a snort. "You're all right, for a girl cat I suppose."

\*\*

A couple of days went by with sightseeing and then on the Saturday Danny decided to play golf at the course not far away. I drove him there and on my return I caught up with washing and ironing, plus some clothing alterations for Danny.

Both cats watched me while I worked.

"I can feel your resentment building, woman!"

"You're right, Reilly. This is almost like being married again!"

"Should I stick my claws in him next time, Mum?" Katie looked at me pleadingly.

That was Katie - always wanting to do the right thing.

"No dear, don't worry. I can put up with this for a bit longer. He's a nice guy really...and decent."

Reilly gave a funny sort of sniff. "You women are all the same - want to mother a man, then when he escapes and you're left with all those tedious chores to do for them, you complain!"

"Shut up, Reilly."

"Why should I? You *like* me talking to you. You've said so in the past. You even wrote a book about me, you love me that much!"

"Yes Reilly, and I mentioned on a number of occasions what a big ego you had too, and that hasn't changed much."

"You can be a nasty woman, woman!"

"And you can be a horrible cat, Reilly."

He blinked at me; one, two, three times, and looked so adorable and funny that I felt all my resentment at my guest disappear like magic.

"Am I? Am I really?"

"Really, Reilly..." I laughed at the words.

"Very musical I must say, but funny, no."

"You make me laugh, cat. Now go away while I get these chores finished. Why don't you and Katie go and play with some gum leaves?"

There was a huge eucalyptus tree at the front of the cottage, the source of many hours of play by neighbourhood kids and my cats, but not all at the same time, fortunately.

"I'd rather watch you steam!"

"But I'm not steaming *now*...well, not much anyway."

"I think I'll pick on Katie."

"No you won't!" I said sternly, but too late - Reilly had already taken a swipe at the little cat.

"Eek! You're a big *beast*, Reilly! I thought you loved me?"

"Don't get those sort of ideas into your head, small cat. This is just a reminder dat I'm still a lot bigger dan you and what's more, I rule da roost around here!"

Katie gazed at him owlishly. "Does that mean you're a rooster?"

"He's cocky enough to be a bantam rooster!" I chipped in.

"You're a nasty woman. I said that before and I'll say it again; nasty, nasty!"

"If you haven't got anything better to do, out you go - you too Katie, but don't let Reilly bully you."

"I try not to, but he's so fast, isn't he?"

"In more ways than one!"

"Eek! I don't want to hear about his old girlfriends!"

"Then I shan't tell you. Off you both go now." I opened the French doors for them and they romped off outside. Katie very smartly leaped over the fence, presumably to visit the neighbours on the other side of my rented cottage. They adored her and had told me on several occasions about how much they loved seeing her. I had noticed that they did not say the same thing about Reilly, however.

I continued with some alterations on a pair of Danny's trousers and then the phone rang. It was my friend Shelley.

"Are you coming to dinner tonight?"

"I don't know Shelley," I replied tiredly. "Danny isn't back from golf yet and I've still got some things to do."

"I wanted to try a new recipe out on you."

"Guinea pig, huh?" I laughed, knowing full well that anything Shelley cooked would be delicious. "I don't know though...oh, here comes Danny now. I can't say much more. Can I call you later?"

"I need to know now, so I can start cooking."

"Er..."

"How about if I tell you Barry will be there too?"

"Er...okay!" Barry was a man with marvelously wicked humour, and added to Shelley's and her husband Kevin's humour, I knew it would be a good evening. I'd had doubts about Danny though, and that's partly the reason why I had procrastinated.

"I'll see you at about six o'clock then," Shelley said and soon after, she rang off.

Danny helped himself to some wine from the fridge and was very chatty. After we'd taken turns at the shower and were on our way to dinner at my friends' house, I realized that Danny had already been drinking before he returned from playing golf. I had a premonition that the evening would not end well.

Over the dinner table Kevin and Barry made droll and witty remarks which were completely lost on Danny who chatted about all sorts of things. Shelley and I exchanged wry glances as Danny carried on chattering away. In the midst of all the humour I thought about my cats, and wondered what they were up to. They'd both had their dinner before we'd left, and had gone outside to places unknown. I hoped they didn't catch any tiny Hamilton frogs while I was out.

At least if I was at home while they caught them, I was able to rescue the dear little frogs and release them safely. It was in the midst of these thoughts that I suddenly remembered the other thing I had to do that night. I had to go to a local pub and write a review on an up and coming "Irish" band. Not one of the members was Irish, but their Irish music was terrific.

After dinner I checked my bag to make sure I'd brought my pens and notebook with me. I didn't relish the evening ahead as I was by now really tired.

"Want some moral support?" Kevin asked me quietly when Danny was busy talking to Barry.

"If you and Shelley could come as well, that would be great." I'd earlier asked Barry if he would like to come along, but he'd declined. Shelley declined the offer too. I believe they'd had enough of Danny's company for the evening.

So off down the street Kevin, Danny and I went, and headed to the pub. At first it was interesting and amusing. Kevin stayed and watched the band as I took notes and Danny wandered off to play pool. He returned to tell us that he'd been talking to a man who was an S.I.S agent. "Are you sure about that?" I asked skeptically, knowing that if the man was indeed the erstwhile agent he'd told Danny he was, then it would be highly unlikely that he would have told him. Danny fervently replied that yes, the man really was an S.I.S man and was telling Danny about his life in the services. "Yeah right," I said, and Danny loped back to the pool table. He returned a couple of times, drunker than ever, made embarrassing comments that other patrons sniggered at, and finally vanished. When it was time to go, we went outside looking for him, after Kevin had first checked out the toilets to ensure he hadn't fallen asleep in there.

I started to worry - Danny was so innocent in many ways that I imagined him being rolled in the gutter out in a back street, his wallet casually lifted from his pocket as if it was nothing.

Kevin and I walked back to their house, in the hope of seeing Danny on the way. We didn't. Barry had gone home and Shelley had gone to bed and was sitting up reading and said no, Danny hadn't returned there. So Kevin and I got in my car and did the rounds of all the pubs, looking for Danny. He was nowhere to be found. We tried the back streets as well, and in the end I told Kevin I had an idea that he might have tried to walk back out to the beach, where I rented my cottage.

I took Kevin back home, checked again with Shelley who was still reading to see if Danny had returned in the meantime, and he hadn't, and so I began a slow drive out to Carter's Beach, casting my gaze from side to side as I drove over the dark main road which headed out past Carter's Beach to Cape Foulwind. At least Danny will be easy to spot, I thought. He was wearing a bold brown and cream wide-striped shirt.

Finally, just as I was about to turn the car into my street, I caught sight of someone in the headlights, weaving from side to side. It was Danny. I gave a toot of the car horn and he stopped and turned, peering into my headlights, then turned back and started weaving his way off to the beach. I called him and he stopped and turned again. When I drew closer he looked scared.

"It's me, Danny," I said. "Come and get in the car."

He wouldn't at first, but by then I was in a very determined mood and was ready to *shove* him in, if necessary, even though he was taller and bigger than me. Although I didn't have far to go, I thought it prudent to get him in the car as there was no telling where he might have wandered off to next.

Maybe my face looked pretty grim after the long day and the harrowing search for him, but surely it wasn't *that* grim, that Danny was too scared to go inside when I told him to? I put my car away in the garage and went to the front door, but Danny was still standing outside, rocking on his feet.

"Come inside," I said in a firm voice, perhaps like one might use on a child who's been in trouble. Danny wouldn't budge, until I grabbed his arm and pulled him inside. He was roaring drunk, and to this day it amazes me that he was able to find his way nearly seven kilometres from the pub we'd been at earlier, back out to Carter's Beach.

Reilly and Katie were at the door, their huge eyes gleaming in the light from the lounge. It was disconcerting. I let them in and Reilly sniffed the air suspiciously.

"Who's been on the booze? Ha, I'm a poet again!"

"How do you know about things like that?"

"What?" said Danny, looking at me strangely through half-closed eyes.

"I was talking to Reilly," I said smoothly, and Danny nodded.

"You'd rather talk to the cats than me?"

"Yes. I'll get more sense out of them," I said bluntly.

"You haven't answered me, woman! Who's been on the booze?"

"Danny has," I said. Danny nodded, and then in his drunken state began to cry.

"You don't know how much I love you!" he declared, and I'd swear I heard Reilly snigger.

"What rubbish!" I said briskly. "You're *drunk,* Danny! I bet by tomorrow you will have forgotten all about this."

"No, no, no, *never!"* he said dramatically and Katie meowed in alarm.

"Take no notice, Katie. Danny's drunk."

"Not too drunk to tell you I *love* you!" he wailed. He leaned back on his chair, rolled sideways and nearly fell off.

I summoned up some patience, made us a cup of coffee each - thinking it didn't matter if it was coffee; it seemed doubtful if I'd get any sleep anyway.

"I'm going to put you to bed!" I said firmly, and that's what I did. Danny's arms waved wildly in the air as I tucked him in like a child. "Woman, will you damn' well marry me?" he shouted at the ceiling.

"No, I damned well won't!" I shouted back. I left the room, deliberately banging the bedroom door. Out in the lounge area the cats were sitting side by side. Katie looked anxious; Reilly looked amused.

I read his expression right.

"He called you woman and asked you to marry him. Who's a *lucky* little woman, den? You got a marriage proposal! Dis is your lucky night! I hope dis don't mean yer gonna leave me and my girlfriend in the lurch!"

"Don't be smart, cat," I said tiredly, but I was amused all the same.

"Oh Reilly, am I really your girlfriend?" Katie piped.

"No, you're a gangster's moll."

"I don't think that sounds very nice at all."

"I'm a tough cat, see? And if you wanna be my bird, you gotta get tough. Get it?"

"I wasn't raised to be like that, you nasty cat!"

"Another poetic cat, huh? Maybe you will do for my moll after all...we do speak a similar language."

"Cats, cats! You can go to bed too! I'm tired."

"You're often tired, woman. I think you gotta health problem."

"Don't tell me what I've got and what I haven't got! Just go to bed, you two!"

And they did. The night had been a far cry from the lovely time we'd had soon after Danny's arrival, when Reilly came for a walk down the beach and Danny took photos - exclaiming all the while about the fascinating cat who liked to have a swim.

"Never seen anything like it before in my life," he'd said in his strong Cockney accent, as Reilly frolicked and swam in the water and gamboled on the beach.

\*\*\*

# CHAPTER SIX

## *Bed Pals*

It was good to finally climb into the bed where I had slept since Danny's arrival. Being a single bed only, there wasn't much room left for me with the cats taking up part of it. How is it that although cats are not big animals, they do seem to have a knack of taking up most of the bed space?

Still, it was wonderful having them there with me, and not even the sound of Danny snoring heavily in the room next door put me off the pleasure of having my warm, clean cats sharing my bed with me. Indeed, I felt privileged that they should want to share it with me. I felt a fierce surge of love for them, a sorrow for their sad background, and happiness that somewhere in the midst of life we had all come together in companionship.

As I began to drift off to sleep I thought about the pleasure in meeting Katie for the first time and how, when I had taken her to the vet in Motueka for her "little operation", the sunny-natured receptionist/nurse was enchanted with my Katie O'Brien, and the coincidence that she, the receptionist, had a cat of exactly the same unique colouring, whom she'd named Tommy Slater.

"Fancy you giving your cat a double-barreled name too!" she'd said, obviously taking pleasure in the coincidence. "It's so rare we get anyone in here with a cat who has two names, especially one like *my* cat!"

Then I thought sleepily of how Reilly had been found - near death and chewing on an old dried out possum skin. My thoughts flickered to neighbours I'd had in Carter's Beach before they moved south. At the time, I had three cats and a pet baby possum which I'd named Boston Henrietta - a rather grandiose name perhaps, but it seemed to suit the wee possum. I thought of my very ample-chested neighbour Biddy visiting, and holding up tiny Boston Henrietta and clucking over her.

"She's due to go to the toilet," I'd said.

"Doesn't matter," Biddy had replied. "She can go in a minute. Who's a dear wee thing, then? Who's Mummy's wee girl?"

"Uh, Biddy..." I'd begun.

She'd looked at me briefly. "What?" Then she'd turned back to Boston Henrietta whom she was holding close to her bosom. "Who's a dear wee girl?"

"Uh - Biddy...wee being the operative word," I'd said firmly.

"What?"

"Boston's peed down the front of your tee-shirt."

"Oh you dirty wee girl!" she'd laughed.

On the left side of Biddy's faded black tee-shirt was a spreading stain. "All over me left boob, too! Never mind, it'll wash."

"I suppose you mean the tee-shirt," I'd said, amused.

"Both! Well, I'd better go and change me shirt."

And off she'd gone, but obviously got involved in other things in the meantime because the next day she'd told me: "when I took me tee-shirt off last night, pooh, I stank of possum wee!"

I wondered what Reilly would have thought about little Boston Henrietta, or more so, what he would have thought about my neighbour. It was easy to picture him sitting with an aloof air, lifting one paw to inspect his claws and saying: "rather disgusting, but very amusing, I'm sure!"

\*\*

It was about that time when I had a mare grazing in my spare section. I became alert again - suddenly remembering. Sleep evading me, I told Reilly about the mare.

Katie opened one eye and went back to sleep.

"Horses for courses," came Reilly's swift reply.

"Just let me tell you the story, Reilly," I said softly.

"Get on with it then woman! What are you waiting for?"

"Well then, stop interrupting me so I can tell you!"

He gave a sniff, washed his paws and looked at me expectantly.

The mare in my spare section was called Twinkletoes and she was about twenty-three years of age. The person who named her must have been hopeful or had a brash sense of humour, as Twinkletoes was a sturdy, chunky little mare with thick hair covered in mare-licks. Somewhere in her background I felt that a lecherous Clydesdale had lurked.

Twinkletoes had a penchant for rolling among the dock leaves, her round tummy blimp-like. I was amused each time I saw her straining her neck over the fence to reach for the grass; inevitably shorter and less tasty-looking that the grass on which she was standing. She truly embraced the old saying about the grass being greener on the other side.

One day I was having a chat to Twinkletoes when her owner joined us, none other than Biddy, who was decked out in old shorts with the stitching coming undone, a tank-top stretched precariously across her enormous bosom, and sandshoes with the toes out of them.

Biddy patted Twinkletoes who was happily chewing grass, her mind a hundred green fields away. Biddy and I chatted about the depressing West Coast unemployment situation, coming to no conclusion except that the situation wasn't improving...but what the heck, it was a lovely day after all.

Twinkletoes backed around to the rickety gate where we were standing. With a bland look in her eyes and (I'd swear) a smile forming, she rubbed her behind obscenely against the gate. Biddy looked on in horror as the gate threatened to collapse. When Twinkletoes lifted her tail, Biddy leaped away; I had never seen her so nimble.

The little mare whinnied and, with no results forthcoming, apart from an enormous, reeking explosion, she let her tail down.

She had most definitely made her opinion known. She rubbed her behind again; the gate creaked - the wire from the straining fence screeched and Biddy looked at me oddly, not knowing what to say. Twinkletoes whinnied again, giving warning of her intentions and let forth with that day's recycled grass. Biddy leaped again and this time slipped on Twinkletoes' recycling efforts, her legs shooting up in the air. I laughed heartily at the sight. Fortunately Biddy laughed too and it was then we decided that it had indeed been a lovely day, despite Biddy having slipped on horse manure and getting her sneakers, bottom and legs in a very dirty, smelly state.

"So what's the moral of the story?"

"There wasn't really a moral to the story. It was just an anecdote...but if you want to make a moral to it, you could say that no matter how bad life seems, you can still count your blessings!"

"I wonder if Biddy did that? Counted her blessings, I mean."

"Possibly. I don't know."

"A horse turns her back on you, obscenely shows off her rear in an insult, farts very loudly and stinkily and threatens to drop a bundle, then does so and you slip over in the mess...and you're supposed to count your blessings?"

"Of course!"

Reilly seemed to smirk. "Yeah, it didn't happen to *you,* thank God!"

I grinned. "You got the picture, cat."

**

I thought about my friend Eve, who'd given me Muffy some years before, and her pet possum which she'd brought along to the clothing factory where we worked. Eve had sat at her sewing machine with her possum lying on top of her head like a Davy Crockett hat. I had asked her what would happen if her pet wanted a wee.

"She'll be right, mate," Eve had said, an oft-heard Kiwi phrase. Soon after, when I saw the spreading stain down her back and I'd grinned broadly, Eve glared and told me not to say a word. I just grinned again and walked away, commenting on the interesting new patterns on the back of her smock.

"Shuddup!" Eve had growled. I wondered what Reilly would think of the situation and what he'd say.

I asked him.

"You just can't trust any old possum, can you? They taste horrible and love to pee. A good combination? I think *not!*"

Finally we drifted off to sleep, to the sound of Danny snoring in the next room.

**

The next morning, the only thing Danny recalled of the previous day's incident were his rounds of golf. I told him what he'd said to me.

"Did I say that? Good Lord! How embarrassing! What did you say?"

"I said a very firm no!" I replied.

"I'm sorry." He looked only slightly repentant and quickly changed the subject to his aching head. I was glad he didn't complain too much about that, because my tolerance level was still pretty low.

On the Monday afternoon Danny's family arrived. Where I was going to squeeze them all in I didn't know, but figured we'd manage somehow. I was getting a bit wound up as I had assignments to do for a South Island-wide newspaper and my deadline for posting was that day at five pm, which meant I had to type them, type out captions for the accompanying photographs, stick them to the back of each photograph and neatly pack everything up. This was in the days just before the enormous convenience of sending everything via email.

The time was drawing close before I had to leave for the Post office, six kilometres away in the township of Westport, and about one less kilometre than Danny had walked just the night before. In the meantime Danny's family arrived, but true to form, Danny told them I wasn't very happy they were there.

His announcement made me feel dreadful as I hadn't said that at all, but had merely said I hoped I could get my work done before they arrived. I soon put them right on what I had actually said, then excused myself to drive into town with my stories all ready to post away.

It was a relief to get in my car and go for a drive, even if I still felt under pressure. Reilly and Katie were nowhere to be seen when Danny's family arrived. It seemed to me that like all cats, their instinct was at work when the household was due to be disrupted, and had made themselves scarce.

On my return home there was another car up my driveway and as I stepped out of my car Shelley opened my French doors and came out to greet me.

"Is there room for everyone inside?" I asked. "How lovely to see you Shelley. I feel normal now, after seeing you!"

"There's just enough room inside," Shelley agreed with a wry grin. "We thought you could do with some moral support."

I was so grateful I gave her a hug. "What about meeting up with us for dinner at Baillie's tonight? I haven't got enough room here to cook for everyone."

"A good idea. I'll tell Kevin. It'll be good for us to have a night out, and anyway, it could be an interesting evening."

It sure was. Shelley told me later she'd never laughed so much in her life and that it was a good tonic for her.

Danny's mum Molly talked in her wonderful Cockney accent about a "weddin' they was goin' ter 'ave", and who might like to be bridesmaids. I was busy fending off small unwanted attentions from Danny, while Kevin baited Danny's Irish Aunty Bridget who kept telling him he was a "daft bleedin' bugger", and Molly's boyfriend Bob took out his false teeth to eat tiny pieces of steak. As Bob already had a speech defect, it made understanding him nigh on impossible. He kind of mumbled his way through the steak and I could feel Shelley quaking with mirth at the highly amusing sight of Bob eating, his false teeth sitting and grinning to one side of his plate.

I say "feel", as I'd been leaning away from Danny and was more or less leaning against Shelley. Her quivering from suppressed mirth was very evident.

Molly, after a very brief silence, began declaring there was such a thing as a shirary.

"Yer daft bugger!" said Bridget. "Dere's no such thing as a shirary."

"I'll ask Amber. She'll know. Amber luv, there is so such a thing as a shirary, isn't there?" Molly pleaded.

"Of course there is!" I said with a grin.

"See Bridget, I *told* yer there were such a thing!"

"An' I say yer a daft pack o' buggers! There ain't no such thing as a shirary!" By then Bridget was practically shouting and others in the restaurant were listening for all their worth and smiling at the free entertainment from our table.

Molly looked at me hopefully. "If Amber sez there's such a thing, then there must be." She paused, scratched her chin then added: "What *is* a shirary, anyway?"

"A hairy *shillelagh*!" I answered with a grin.

Shelley, sitting to the left of me, cried with laughter and nearly fell off her chair.

I wondered what Reilly would have thought of this carry-on.

"You're all a daft pack of buggers, just like the woman Bridget said," I imagined Reilly saying - with that superior look he was so fond of assuming.

Meanwhile, Bob went on gnawing and mumbling away at his tiny bits of steak and Molly continued chattering about "'oneymoons", and I continued trying my best to lean away from Danny, who by then, had had several drinks more and his intentions were very clear.

**

Kevin and Shelley, still chuckling at the night's events went home and the rest of us went back to my cottage.

"What about readin' us some o' yer poetry, luv?" Molly asked me.

"I'd be happy to and I'll do it by candlelight." In the meantime, I hoped, Danny would be ready to doze off and would stop trying to make not-so-subtle advances.

"Ooh, luvly! Do y' hear that, Bridget? Amber's going to read us poetry by candlelight!"

"Oh good! I ain't finished with der evening yet!" Bridget replied. "No, not by a long shot, indeed no."

Bob mumbled something encouraging. I wondered if he still had tiny bits of steak in his mouth.

Although it was late, I set up the table with a big multi-coloured candle in the middle and turned out the lights. Reilly's and Katie's eyes gleamed from one of the sofas.

"Not having a seance, are you? That's against my religion!"

"It's against mine too, Reilly," I said.

"What was that, luv? Is that the name of the poem?" Molly looked puzzled, but very humorous, since the burning candle caused rays of light to reflect off her glasses and made her glasses seem like little headlights.

"No, I was talking to the cat," I explained.

"I suppose yer think he answers yer back an' all," Bridget said dryly.

I merely agreed with her. "Of course."

"You writers are a daft pack of buggers!" she responded.

It seemed to me that in Bridget's book, any group of people was likely to fall prey to the title of "a daft pack of buggers"!

"Hurry up woman! I want to hear dis poetry of yours."

"Okay, okay I'm ready, but I demand silence from everyone - absolute silence!" I said bossily.

"Silence in the court, the monkey wants to talk!"

"Be quiet, Reilly!"

"Huh? I didn't hear anything," Danny said, turning sleepily to look at a smug-looking Reilly.

"Nor did I," said Bridget.

"That's just in case he makes a noise," I amended, narrowing my eyes at Reilly. Even in the gloom and flickering shadows cast by the candlelight, Reilly appeared to have a self-satisfied look.

"Poor pussycat," Molly said, getting out of her chair to go over to Reilly who had suddenly assumed a hurt, offended air.

"I'll speak to you later, Reilly," I growled, then turned my gaze back to those at the table. Molly patted Reilly and returned to the table to sit down again and finally everyone was quiet. I launched into my poetry and to my pleasure they all enjoyed it.

"You didn't like *my* poetry, woman!"

"What about your poetry?"

"What poetry?" The others echoed and looked at me, puzzled.

"Silence in the court, the monkey wants to talk!" Reilly said again and sniggered.

"That's old, old stuff. I heard that when I was a kid!"

"What? Are yer saying yer didn't write the poetry you just read to us?" Bridget demanded.

"Of course I wrote it! I was talking to my cat!"

"You're all bloody barmy over here on the Coast!" Bridget snapped.

Molly yawned and got to her feet. "I'm tired. Coming ter bed, luv?" she asked Bob.

"Uh," he grunted and off they went to my bedroom. I'd managed to find time earlier to make up the bed again. Bridget, I'd decided before their arrival, could have my bed in the office and Danny and I would each have a sofa in the lounge to sleep on. I was pretty sure that I would be safe from any advances Danny might make: Reilly made an excellent guard cat.

But Danny's energy returned and he and his Aunty Bridget began to argue and Bridget, with several wines under her belt became very maudlin and started to cry. By then it was two o'clock in the morning and I felt like a zombie. I left Danny and Bridget to their old family arguments and separated the two sofas and pushed one out into the centre of the lounge area.

Bridget forgot her woes for a moment to ask me what I was doing.

"Getting our beds ready," I said briskly.

"Where will your pussycats sleep?"

"Danny and I can have one each," I replied as I placed crocheted blankets and thick patchwork rugs over each sofa.

"Look luv, the girl wants us ter go ter bed..." said Bridget, her good humour restoring itself.

"We've all had a big day," I said easily, thinking, *bigger than most.*

\*\*\*

# CHAPTER SEVEN

## *Retreat From The Enemy*

Soon after, Bridget went to bed in my office and Danny and I settled down with a cat each on the makeshift beds. I'd moved an armchair to the end of the arm-less sofa on which Danny was to sleep, to give him extra leg-room. It worked well.

As for me, I didn't need a chair for extra length as I'm not very tall.

Danny lay down with Katie; I had Reilly. All was quiet in the early hours of the morning until Danny let out a loud snore. Reilly got such a fright that he sunk his claws into me as traction to make as fast a getaway as possible.

"Help! The enemy is coming! Retreat! Retreat!"

I retreated - under the blankets to shut out the din of Danny's snoring and to nurse my sore arm where Reilly had sunk his claws. Katie scrambled off the sofa where Danny slept and leaped onto me, her eyes extra-huge in the half-light.

"I'm scared! I'm scared!"

"Retreat, everyone!"

"Shut up you two," I said quietly. "It's only Danny snoring."

"Snoring, eh? I thought it was something from the Second World War!"

"How could you possibly know that, cat? Even *I* was born long, long after the war was over!" I whispered fiercely.

"Which one? The Boer War?"

"No, you naughty cat. World War Two."

"Did you cause it?"

"How could I? As I said before, I was born long, long after the war was over! Anyway, what would you know about the war?"

"You forget, woman, that we cats, being the superior creatures we are, retain memories passed down from one generation to the next."

"Several generations of pussycats still isn't necessarily a long time!" I retorted.

"I'm not talking about several generations...I'm talking about hundreds of years!"

"Oh," I said softly. "You're a much older pussycat that I thought."

"Do be quiet, woman! I'm trying to get some sleep!"

"Cheeky cat," I whispered. "On the retreat again, eh? I thought you were a tough cat?"

"Who of us are tough when the bombs are falling, woman - answer me *that!*"

"Are bombs falling? Good heavens, how could I not have heard them? Funny, all I heard was snoring."

Katie hopped out from under my blankets. Danny was still asleep, blissfully snoring still, but at least the decibels were less.

"I can't bear it when you two argue. Please can we get some sleep?"

"That's what I've been trying to get this woman to do - but you know how it is Katie, humans are a contrary species...and boy, they sure do frighten easily!"

"You lie!" I whispered loudly.

But Reilly was already closing his eyes again and, cunning cat that he is, had let Katie, who was delighted at his apparent friendliness towards her, snuggle up beside him. There was barely room for me to move.

Reilly had won the round again.

It was hard to go back to sleep with two purring cats and also being aware of Danny's, by now, softer snoring. I thought of the fact that Reilly now purred quite often, which he did not do much for the first eighteen months or so of his life.

I felt as if someone had flung sand into my eyes – they felt that gritty. I thought back to the move to Motueka some months before. Friend Keith had moved my furniture the three and a half hour trip northwards, with his son and his son's friend helping. By that night we were all very tired. Since Keith is a big man, I had told him he could use my large bed and off he went to sleep first. Reilly and I had the single bed in the spare bedroom while the boys slept on the sofas in the lounge. It was quiet until around five am, when Reilly and I were woken with a shock at a terrible kind of short, sharp and loud buzzing sound. My heart had pounded with fright and I guess Reilly's must have been pounding too. In the early morning light his great eyes were wide and staring, and he had adopted a rigid-legged pose.

"Are we at war?"

"Sounds like it," I'd said. We both waited for the next onslaught and then it came, an even more shattering sound...and then I realized what it was. Keith had let out two of the loudest snores I have ever heard...and possibly am ever likely to hear.

"If dis is what marriage could mean, den I'm off the idea already!"

"I didn't know pussycats got married," I'd said amusedly, my heart settling into a more normal rhythm.

"We have our ways and means!"

"I'm sure you have," I'd replied.

He'd peered into my face, his eyes fixed on something. Just in time I realized what it was...the movement of my blinking eyes. I'd been caught that way many years before when a cat of mine batted at my eyelashes and caught me, very painfully, in one eye.

**

I figured I'd had about three hours' sleep in total when I was woken at around seven am by Molly getting up and talking to herself. She went to the tiny bathroom just through the wall from where I was snuggled with my cats on the second sofa and ran the shower. The old pipes shuddered and banged, and Molly clattered and thumped around. She emerged a few minutes later, opened the door by my head and banged the door shut and then, still talking to herself, she pulled the drapes back. They were noisy on their metal rings. Both my cats glared at her and I felt like glaring too, except that my eyes were too sore to open immediately.

Molly went to the sink, banged the electric jug against the tap and turned the tap on with a great spurt and muttered loudly.

"Good morning Molly," I said tiredly.

"Oh, did I wake yer, luv?" she said innocently.

"Wake us! *Wake* us! The woman is *demented*, I say!"

"She means well, Reilly," Katie piped, her green eyes enormous and sad.

"*Means* well, you daft cat! As far as you are concerned, *everyone* means well! You're too nice for your own good, Katie O'Brien."

"Oh Reilly, you can be so sweet to me at times!"

"Now don't go all soppy over me this morning. I'm in a bad mood. I'm not ready to wake up. Grrr...leave me alone so I can get back to sleep!"

But Molly started chattering and Danny woke up.

"No rest for the wicked, Reilly," I said cheekily. I stuck my head back under the blankets.

"And wicked is what I think I will be today. Just you watch me!"

"Oh Reilly, I'm too tired for your nonsense!"

"O'Reilly, dat's me! And I'm in a bad mood everyone...so just keep outa me way! Dat means you too, Katie O'Brien!"

"What did I do wrong?" she piped plaintively.

"Nuttin...just being you is enough!"

"Stop it you two," I said sternly. Katie gave me a reproachful look and I immediately smiled at her and gave her a cuddle. She purred noisily.

"I didn't hear them fighting," Danny yawned.

"Nor did I," his mother chipped in.

"They're exchanging words," I said, my eyes narrowed against the glare of the early morning sunlight.

"She thinks she can understand them," Danny said, yawning again.

"Maybe she can," Molly agreed, and banged around in the tiny kitchen area.

"She probably hears things that go bump in the night, too!" Danny laughed derisively.

"I do...*you!*" I said. "You sounded like a traction engine starting up."

"That's a sign of me having a good sleep," he replied, unconcerned about his loud snoring.

"Glad at least *some* of us slept well," I said sourly. "How did you sleep, Molly?"

"Oh fine, luv," she said.

"Everybody but me," I grouched quietly. My nerves felt very raw indeed.

"And me!" said Reilly.

"And me too!" piped dear little Katie.

"Never mind my pets, you can sleep later," I said softly.

"Huh? But I had a good sleep," said Molly.

"And so did I," said Danny.

"I was talking to my cats," I said.

Danny gave me a wary, narrowed look. "You'll get a shock one day when they answer you back!"

"They already do," I said smugly.

Danny and his mother exchanged knowing glances, but I didn't care. Let them think what they would. I had a rapport with my cats which I was proud of, and many people simply would not understand that rapport.

"I'm up and off to be a bad cat!" Reilly informed me as he stretched and yawned. I glared at him. He smirked and swiped at my moving hand as I pulled the blankets back. "Here's a start!"

My hand smarted. I patted Reilly's fluffy bottom and with a chirrup, he was out of bed and off to make an attempt to climb up the drapes.

"Reilly!" I shouted. "Don't you dare!"

# Catmopolitan Critic

"Paper? No thanks — got some!"

He gave me a look as much to say: how can you speak to a cat such as me - like that? Instead of flinging himself at the drapes as he was wont to do, he sharpened his claws on the carpet. *Thwock! Thwock!* The sound was loud in the still morning air. Molly had temporarily come to a halt with her clattering and banging around, to watch Reilly and his antics. He tore at magazines on the coffee table; they fell off and Reilly proceeded to tear covers off them at great speed. Within a few minutes he had a mess on the floor - tattered bits of magazine were all over the lounge floor. He slid under the coffee table, taking bits of the magazines with him and proceeded to chew them up and spit out the bits of glossy paper.

"You can go out, Reilly. You've got far too much energy for this time of day, my lad."

"I'll go when I'm ready. And I'm not ready yet."

I opened the French door. "Out you go." Reilly attacked my leg on the way out.

"Take that, woman! Didn't you hear a word I said?"

"Ouch! So much for the rapport I thought we had!"

"Serves you right. Just to spite you now, I'm off and out. I think I'll go and pick on Misty."

"Do, by all means," I said sourly, looking back to where Katie was still sitting on the sofa, looking anxious.

"He's a bad cat, Mum, but so handsome."

"The worst ones usually are!"

Molly and Danny exchanged glances again, and I decided it was time to keep my mouth shut.

Reilly went off with a chirrup and a flick of his tail, and a few minutes later I heard him arguing with Misty, next door's bad-tempered ginger cat. I couldn't help but think that while he was busy arguing with Misty, at least he was using up some of his excess energy. I watched them for a moment, wondering what Reilly would have made of Honeybelle of Mandalay, one of the cats I'd had when I first moved to the West Coast.

Honeybelle was a feisty, ginger kitten and I had euphemistically given her a fancy name in the hope it would improve her nature. It didn't, but I had to give her full marks for personality.

Anything red or feathered was possible food and anyone who tried to take red wool or red fabric off her - or even feathers such as the ones off my operatic society hat - was fiercely growled at and generally warned to keep their distance. If Honeybelle was awake at four am, then I had to be too, and if I didn't wake up then I was hit in the face.

Being hit in the face with sharp claws at four am is not conducive to further sleep. I wore the scar for over two years. For several days following the incident Honeybelle was so well-behaved she seemed too good to be true...which she usually was. It was almost as if she was thinking: *I'll wait until Mum cools down before I start being naughty again.*

But months of scratched legs and hands, visitors attacked and pot plants attacked and subsequently ruined became too much, even for a softy like me. I put an ad in the local newspaper: "wanted, kind and loving home for spayed, extremely active nine-month old red tabby cat, loaded with personality."

A friendly lady telephoned, keen to have Honeybelle. She arrived in her little car, excited in her movements as she got out, and her eyes lit up even further when she saw Honeybelle. I told the lady that Honeybelle had even made the New Zealand Woman's Weekly Pet of the Week page. She was thrilled and happily took Honeybelle away with her. Two days later I'd phoned and a somewhat subdued new owner told me that Honeybelle had knocked an heirloom bottle of wine off a top shelf.

"I had no idea she could manage to get up there - the shelf's near the ceiling."

I refused to feel guilty. After all, my ad had said Honeybelle was very active and full of personality, and I had reiterated those points very clearly to the lady when she came to take charge of her new cat.

"Now, Honeybelle is very feisty and full of energy," I'd warned the lady.

"I just love ginger cats," she'd said simply, ignoring my warning. Some weeks later I saw the lady and her sister outside a local supermarket. Both seemed subdued and both of them had arms covered in scratches. Honeybelle was living up to her ad.

So why did I persist with Reilly, who was every bit as bad as Honeybelle? Worse, even? I don't know. The wild cat was obviously in both of them - but most likely the deciding factor of finding a new home for Honeybelle was because she kept picking on my sweet, good-natured tortoiseshell cat Muffy.

Reilly at least had the opportunity of growing into adulthood before other cats came on the scene. But in his case, he did not grow up into a mellow cat - oh no, he was that much worse, because he was a lot bigger! And a big cat can demolish a pot plant a lot faster than a kitten can.

On this particularly morning he appeared to become bored at arguing under the fence with Misty, so he leaped to the top and hurled obscenities down to him. I could hear them clearly, only vaguely aware of Danny and Molly watching me watching the cats.

"You is a fat, disgusting cat!"

"Who do you think you are, bossing me around when I was here first!"

"I'll say whatever I like. Dis is my territory now, you fat, ginger, disgusting cat!"

"I'm gonna tell my human. And what's more, I'm gonna bale up your girlfriend and beat her up!"

"Dat's because you're a bully. If I catch you picking on my girl, you'll have *me* to answer to - me, the Grey Ghost of Carter's Beach."

"What an ego. You don't scare me!"

"You'll be sorry. Dis is my territory and Katie is my girl."

"Just you watch me come on over, Bud."

Under the fence he came and Reilly flung himself at him. As Misty wasn't expecting this tactic he screamed with injured pride and I had to open the door again and yell at Reilly. He turned around and Misty took the opportunity to quickly disappear back under the tall fence. Reilly had a tuft of ginger fur in his mouth and looked hilarious.

"That colour suits you!" I remarked.

"Yeah. Especially in my mouth! I've just warned him off Katie and off my territory," he said while spitting out tufts of ginger fur.

"I know, I heard you clearly. Good boy," I said, smoothing down his fur which was still sticking out in anger.

Katie came to greet him and smooched against him.

"My hero!" she purred.

"Ergh! Gerroff!"

But he looked pleased all the same and Katie leaped back onto the sofa, purring happily, her big green eyes half-shut. If I didn't already know what a sweet little cat she is, I'd have accused her of having wicked thoughts about Reilly.

Danny and his mother exchanged a few more knowing glances and rolled their eyes. I began to feel fed up with them; in fact, the whole family.

"I suppose you think that Reilly talks to that ginger cat?" Molly said.

"He does indeed and he doesn't like him one bit."

Danny and Molly both snorted in amusement. If I hadn't known better I would have said they had been practicing their derisive snorts, to keep them in unison. My sour mood didn't lighten, although I did my best to stay cheerful, at least on the surface.

***

# CHAPTER EIGHT

## *Bad Intentions*

My other visitors emerged from my bedroom and my office and yawned sleepily. Somehow in the very confined space I managed to prepare breakfast for us all. Their intention was to drive down the Coast, stay a night or two en route, then cross the island back to Christchurch before staying overnight at Bridget's house. Bridget had moved to New Zealand from Ireland about five years earlier. The others were to fly back to England the next day.

They asked to have a look at Ruby, my car; my two-tone red and deep charcoal 1978 Mazda RX7, with spoilers at the front and rear. With her two-tone body, mag wheels, wide tyres and spoilers, Ruby was a very sleek looking little sports car and I was very fond of her. I had been to many remote places in her, in the course of my job as a freelance journalist. I consider that I have been to many places in New Zealand that most wouldn't see in a lifetime.

"What a lovely car!" Molly exclaimed, turning to look at her son. "You must 'ave enjoyed coming back from Christchurch in 'er!"

"Oh I did Mum!" Danny enthused.

"I 'ope you didn't go too fast," Molly added, turning to look sternly at me.

"Oh no," I said with an innocent look. "Never over 100 kilometres an hour on the open road, just like I told a cop once when he asked me how fast Ruby would go!"

But Molly wasn't really listening. She glanced down at Reilly, who had come to see what was going on in the garage, and then glanced back at me. The garage was crowded. I felt crammed up against the garbage bin. Molly frowned as if there was something she wanted to say, but didn't know how to say it.

Then it came in a rush.

"I want ter know what yer intentions are towards me son."

I felt a great bubble of mirth rise up and threaten to escape, as I'd been looking down at the garbage bin at the time of Molly's comment, and I almost said "rubbish". I held the mirth down, just, and told Molly what Danny had said to me in the early hours of the previous Sunday morning.

"Oh I don't blame yer then luv, fer refusin' 'im."

I looked down again at the garbage bin, hiding a smile.

"It's all a load of old rubbish anyway," Reilly observed with a leer. "Not much of a proposal, and fancy having his mother ask you *your* intentions!"

"Yes it *is* amusing, isn't it?" I said out loud.

Molly looked at me strangely. "You'd be very lucky to get my Danny all the same!" she said darkly.

"*Un*lucky! Reilly sniggered. "I *told* you that you needed me around!"

"How could I forget? You remind me often enough," I said, looking sternly at him.

"What?" said Molly, and the others looked strangely at me as well. I was suddenly aware of the glances.

"What? Oh...nothing, just thinking aloud about something..."

"Were not," said Reilly.

"Were too," I responded, and earned more strange looks from the others. I wondered later if they were thinking it was just as well I had turned down Danny's proposal - or maybe it was really the other way round and he'd turned down a proposal from *me! The way the young woman talks to herself when she looks at her cats...well, we just don't know about her...something weird here,* I could imagine them thinking.

Reilly padded away to join Katie who was busy going to the toilet in my garden. Reilly bopped her with a fluffy paw in passing.

"Eek! You spied on me Reilly! Go away. You shouldn't be watching a lady cat going about her toilet!"

"You shouldn't go in such a public place, den. Lookit all dem people looking at you!"

Katie's head swivelled around and she saw us all looking.

"Eek!"

Reilly snickered as he rounded the corner to go back inside the cottage. It was only after Reilly had gone inside when I remembered that he'd cheeked me about "who's a lucky little woman, den?" in reference to Danny's dubious marriage proposal. So Reilly had since changed his mind. "Wherever the wind bloweth," he'd said to me once, "there bloweth I."

I had accused him of being a little windbag with divided loyalties.

He had simply given me a lofty look and walked away muttering something about it being his prerogative to change his mind about something whenever it suited him. Which was practically every day.

**

After everyone had left, except me and the cats of course, the cottage seemed oddly quiet. But I felt as if a huge burden had lifted, with the departure of my visitors. The phone shrilled in the silence. It was Shelley.

"Have you been holding out on me? Is there something you haven't told me that you should have?" she asked. I could hear laughter in her voice.

"About what?"

"You didn't tell me you were getting married, let alone going to England for your honeymoon!"

"What wedding? What honeymoon? Who am I supposed to be getting married to?"

"Danny, you daft thing. Didn't you know?" She laughed.

I laughed too. "No I didn't. Just as well you told me, otherwise I would never have known!" I told her about Danny's dubious, drunken proposal and she asked me why I hadn't queried the comments from Molly about an "'oneymoon" when we were at Baillies Restaurant the previous night.

"I was too busy trying to lean away from Danny, and explain to his mother what a shirary was."

Shelley gave me some more cheek about holding out on her on my wedding plans. "Didn't you wonder what Molly was going on about with the honeymoon?"

"I thought she was talking about her daughter's honeymoon." Molly's daughter had got married only a few months before.

"No, it was supposed to be *yours*, silly! Fancy not knowing about your own wedding!"

I laughed again and told her about another incident a few years before when a friend rang to tell me he'd heard some really interesting news. I'd asked him what the news was. Joe's getting married in April, he'd replied. Well, well, fancy that, I'd remarked. I'd added that I hoped he'd be very happy but I thought it was strange that Joe hadn't said anything to me about it, particularly as I'd seen a great deal of the whole family and had done numerous chores to help them along on life's path.

You'd never guess who he's getting married to, the friend had said. Who? I'd asked. *You*, came the triumphant reply. Well, I'll be a stunned mullet, I'd said, laughing. Fancy not telling *me!* Fancy, the friend had said - amusement in his voice. Obviously it was all a load of bull, he'd added. You got that right, I'd said firmly, knowing the family's penchant with regularly getting into serious trouble with the law. Also obvious, was the fact that that family's members had a penchant of making up stories that were not true. I thought congratulations were in order, my friend had added. Not bleedin' likely! I had retorted.

"Looks like it's all happened again, Shelley said. "You'd better be careful Amber. One day you might find yourself up the aisle and married before you realize it!"

"That'll be the day," I said darkly.

"It just might be!" Shelley laughed and rang off. It seemed highly likely that Danny had been discussing possible wedding plans with his family without barely having met me, let alone *asking* me! It was more déjà vu for me.

"Still think you're a lucky little woman, den?" Reilly suddenly appeared from presumably the bathroom.

"Yes, to have made a lucky escape. Anyway, where did *you* spring from?"

"Da toilet, dear woman. Der water tastes far better dan outa me bowl."

"For a cat who prides himself on his good looks etcetera, you can be a right little grub at times."

"I gotta keep you guessing. I can't have you knowing all my ways in advance."

"Sometimes you can be so profound, cat."

He narrowed his eyes. "Are you being sarcastic?"

I tried to look innocent, but a grin broke through. "Who, me? No," I said, the grin spreading.

"I thought you were supposed to be a lady. Ladies are never sarcastic...they are genteel...always."

"Oh yeah? Sez who?"

"Me, the Grey Wise One. Have you heard dis joke?"

"I don't know until you tell me..." I began, but he interrupted me.

"Quiet, while I concentrate! There's this guy you see..."

"I have seen lots of guys..."

"Don't interrupt me!"

"Yes, your highness," I said, bowing deeply.

"Dis guy says to the other one: who was dat lady I saw you wid last night? And the other one says, dat was no lady, dat was my wife!"

"Oh very funny...ha ha. I've heard that joke many times, and several times from *you*. Yet another old chauvinistic joke against women!"

"It wouldn't sound as funny if it was the other way round. What if I had said: who was dat man I saw you wid last night? And da woman said, dat was no man, dat was my husband!"

"Now *that's* very funny!"

He looked at me sourly. "You just *had* to say dat, didn't you?"

"How about *dat*, fat cat! Oh yes, that's right, you're the Grey Wise One, or the Grey Ghost or The Caped One of Carter's Beach! I *mustn't* forget who you are."

Reilly glared at me and, with a sudden arrogant look, he swept past me with all the grandeur of the high-born and went into my bedroom. Sulking now, I thought. He didn't like it when I occasionally had the last word.

As if to punctuate my thoughts, there came the unmistakable *thwock! Thwock!* as he ran around the outside of my mattress base, chirruping happily as he went.

It was as if he was making the statement: Dat'll learn ya!

When in doubt, either sit down for a wash or make a statement; that could have been his motto.

**

Still, I had my own methods of having the last word, metaphorically speaking.

I'd noticed Reilly scratching on a few occasions of late, so while he was busy making a statement on my mattress base, I reached for the can of flea spray, quietly took the lid off and hid the can behind some folded-up clothes on top of the washing machine.

"Reilly, come out of the bedroom!" I called.

"What for?"

*Thwock! Thwock!*

"I've got something nice for you."

*Thwock!*

"Oh yeah?"

*Thwock!*

"Yeah...come and get it!" I called, sing-song. He emerged and looked around the room, highly suspicious.

"I don't see anything out of the ordinary."

"Come here my lovely pussycat."

"There's gotta be a catch to this. Where's Katie?"

"She's outside somewhere."

"Why isn't *she* here, having a treat too?"

"Reilly, I didn't know you cared!"

With a swift movement I picked him up, whisked up the can of flea spray, opened the back door and bent down to get him in a firm grip.

"Hiss! Get off me, woman!"

He struggled, hissed and growled. It never ceased to amaze me at how much strength there was in him. I sprayed as quickly as possible and ran my fingers through his fur.

"This won't take long..."

"Arrgh! I thought you said you had a treat for me! Never again will I trust a human being!"

I finished the job, washed my hands and looked out to see Reilly leap away to the back fence where he turned to face me with a glare.

"You betrayed me!"

"Nonsense! You had fleas and they would have only got worse. You should be grateful!"

"*Grateful?* For *that?* You must have rocks in your head! Go away and let me suffer in peace."

He began to scratch again as the few fleas tried to get away from the spray which, after all, was very pleasantly scented. He should have been grateful for that fact too, as flea sprays so often smelled horrible.

"Reilly, come and have your treat."

"Don't want it. It's probably something else poisonous. And I thought you *loved* me!"

"Oh but Reilly, I do. That's why I had to do this. Now...come and have a treat."

"Haven't you heard? I don't want it."

"Okay, you don't want any whipped cream. That's okay by me. You're a bit overweight anyway."

I took the lid off the can of whipped cream. It made an interesting *pock* sound.

Reilly raced inside with a chirrup. "Gimme! Gimme!"

He lapped at the swirl of cream I'd squirted into his bowl and turned his head to me, his whiskers covered in cream. With a sudden movement he leaped at me and bit my leg in two places.

"*Ow!* You awful cat! What was that for?"

"One: you betrayed me, and two: you called me overweight. How dare you? I am in the peak of health." He turned back to his bowl and finished off the cream and began to purr.

I felt as if he'd had the last word after all. And that was something he often had.

\*\*\*

# CHAPTER NINE

## *The Answer Lies In The Soil*

One weekend soon afterwards I had several visitors call in to see me and while we were all talking and generally relaxing, we idly looked out the French door to watch Reilly. Our attention was soon gained when he began digging in the sandy ground and sand went flying. It made an amusing arc in the air and Reilly looked funny as well. Even from several metres away we could see damp sand stuck to his whiskers and ear tufts. His head appeared to be almost twice its normal size.

He perched over the hole he'd dug. I opened the door and called to him, doing my best not to laugh.

"Have you no shame, Reilly?"

He spun around and glared. Indeed, he was very impressive, with that glare and his head almost twice its size. He looked like a miniature lion.

"How dare you watch me like that?"

"You told Katie not to go to the toilet in a public place," I reminded him.

"I am a firm believer in do as I say, not as I do. Now, avert your eyes, woman!"

Fortunately, the friends with me were well aware of my chats with my cats, and were amused rather than wary of a possibly dotty woman. I watched Reilly neatly scratch over his business and then stare down at the slightly heaped pile where he'd left his mark.

I wondered what he'd espied.

"What are you doing?" I called. I heard quiet chuckling from my visitors and some murmured comments.

"I'm staring at the ground."

*What else?*

"You weird cat. Why?"

"I think the answer lies in the soil!"

I laughed and repeated it to my visitors.

"What an imagination you have, Amber."

I just smiled to myself and opened the door for my big cat. "Where's Katie?"

"Over at the neighbour's. I want her to see my alter-ego."

"Which one is that?"

Reilly pranced around the room and clawed the tea towel off the handrail on the oven. It was a neat, clever little act of his to drape the tea towel over his back and run away with it. He looked hilarious.

"Let me out the door. I want to show Katie!"

I opened it and out he ran. My visitors laughed heartily. "He's weird!" they chorused.

"The Caped One strikes again!" Reilly called gleefully from outside.

"As long as you don't strike Katie," I said - the door still open to ensure he heard me.

"Huh?" said one of my visitors, not quite understanding this time.

"He said that the Caped One strikes again."

"Oh yeah sure, Amber," my visitors said, almost in unison.

Off Reilly went, down the driveway, around the corner and up the neighbour's driveway. Presently I heard laughter from over there and Katie's piping little voice.

"My hero!"

"Yeah, dat's me, baby. The Caped Cat strikes again!"

It would have looked better if, say, the tea towel was plain or was striped, but the few bold daisies on it spoiled the effect somehow. Or maybe that was part of the Caped One's plan. Possible enemies would be too busy laughing, their eyes shut with that laughter and that's when Reilly would strike. What a cunning, devious cat!

Just as cunning was the thought that possible enemies would be bamboozled as to Reilly's motives for attack. From my point of view, he never needed a motive for anything. If the mood was on him to do something...then he did it.

My visitors left, still chuckling over Reilly's antics and some time later both Reilly and Katie returned. The tea towel was missing.

"Where's your cape, O Esteemed One?" I asked.

He sat at the door and seemed to huff on his claws.

"Oh, that old rag? It's served its purpose. I want my next cape to be in black velvet."

"Ooooh Reilly, you would look *so* handsome!"

He looked smug. "I'm handsome anyway, but even I have to admit that a black velvet cape would add a certain panache."

"Anyway Reilly, what were you staring at in the garden earlier?"

"When I said the answer lies in the soil?"

"Yes, that."

He leered. "Go and dig it up and see for yourself, and therein lies your answer!"

"Oh very *clever*, cat!"

Katie leaped back onto the sofa, snuggled into the rug I'd crocheted, and purred contentedly. Reilly sat just inside the door and chewed at the claws on his front paws, then spat out the sheaths onto the carpet.

"That's not nice."

"Gotta spit dem out somewhere. Just be grateful I didn't spit dem into your cup of coffee, woman!"

"Sometimes you are a revolting cat, Reilly."

"Re-volting, dat's me! Da Caped Cat revolts! Dis is a revolution!"

"Hmmm, maybe I could paint your claws pink while you're sleeping."

"Are you mad? *Pink?* Arrgh! I haven't forgotten you putting a pink flannel on da corner of da bath for me to sit on."

"Better than that cold enamel on your behind."

"Why can't you have a bath here? I *liked* getting into the bath with you."

"Maybe the next place we're at, Reilly. Shall I put in a special request for you?"

He lowered his head and looked at me suspiciously.

"Are you being sarcastic, woman?"

"Who, me?" I assumed an innocent air. "Now, about the colour pink — it's one of my favourites you know, and it's the colour of love."

"How ghastly!"

"I painted the toenails of this guy once, who wasn't a very nice person. He'd come for a visit and had fallen asleep on my sofa. It made the job easy, the fact that he was wearing open sandals. Gosh, the pink varnish did look funny with his hairy toes!"

"I should puke, I should."

"If you must puke, do it outside. Anyway, as I was saying, I painted his toenails and he didn't even notice when he woke up. His father came around to give him a ride home and laughed, but didn't say anything right away. Here were these two big guys yabbering on about facets of engineering, and one of them had bright pink toenails!"

"I suppose you got tossed over the wall when it was discovered what you had done?"

"Oh no! I looked innocently at them and said a little gremlin must have done it, but I removed myself smartly all the same, and went out into the kitchen."

"Just don't get it into your head that you can do the same thing to me."

"You've got hairy toes too, cat," I grinned.

"*Furry*, woman, furry is the word!" It sounded like a line from a song from the musical "Grease" and I was tempted to sing it, but I didn't feel like any more smart remarks from Reilly, for the time being, anyway.

Katie piped at him from the cosiness of the sofa.

"Reilly, come and sit with me please. I'm lonely."

"Women! Mushy, soppy things, so they are."

But he hopped up onto the sofa anyway and I watched Katie give him a loving wash. Of course Reilly only allowed that because he thought I wasn't watching. I'd turned away and was watching with what my mother would have referred to as "half an eye".

\*\*

Later that day a breeze sprung up, perfect for getting my washing dry. Reilly was outside prancing around under the clothesline, enjoying taking mock swipes at the flapping clothes.

"Arghh! Dis is a duel. A *duel,* I say!"

A sudden stiff gust of wind neatly lifted some of my clothes off the line, the pegs clattering on the concrete below. A pair of pink satin and lace knickers fell on Reilly's head.

"I can't see! I can't see! Dis is totally undignified for a cat such as myself...wait a minute...this satin is rather sensuous...but gimme another colour! You *know* I hate pink!"

"Goodie, you can have them to match your claws - that's when I get to paint them," I suggested with a smile, earning myself a black look from a leg opening in the knickers.

When I had stopped laughing, Reilly extricated himself with as much dignity as he could muster and said: "well really, when you think of it, a cat such as I should only be in contact with the most *elegant* of fabrics!"

\*\*

I was in bed reading when I heard a distinctive sound which I knew came from a tiny and very rare Hamilton tree frog in trouble. As both my cats were outside I guessed they'd baled up the little frog. I got out of bed, donned my slippers and a jacket and out the back I went.

REILLY — THE WIND-UP CAT

"SATIN'S NiiiICE! UNDERWEAR'S O.K.!! BUT WIND...

There were my cats – totally at one with each other, both sitting the same way and occasionally tapping gently at the frog. I managed to rescue the tiny amphibian unharmed. I took it inside and called my cats in. As soon as they were inside I stepped back out, shut the door behind me and released the little frog in long, cool grass as far away at the back of the section as possible.

I really felt as if I had done a good deed for the day. I returned to the cottage and gave my bare feet a quick wash before heading back to bed and my book.

**

When birds managed to get into the ceiling cavity from time to time it was just as well that Katie was usually away visiting the neighbours and Reilly was out exploring. There was a gap between the guttering and just under the eaves which the landlord had allowed for ventilation. That was not always practical on the West Coast, which has a very high rainfall. Sturdy leaves from the eucalyptus tree would blow into the guttering and when heavy rain fell the inevitable happened: the guttering became blocked and overflowed; some of the water running down the side of the guttering and the other going into the ceiling.

Early one morning at around one o'clock I heard a steady drip, drip begin, and even getting out of bed and putting a sponge in the bottom of a plastic bucket underneath the leak to help deaden the sound didn't work all that well.

I rang the landlord just after breakfast to tell him and late that morning he arrived to fix the problem – in his own peculiar way. He entered my bedroom with a small sturdy stepladder, hand drill, and an old plastic bucket. He jammed the ugly old bucket against the side of my bed to catch water as it fell, climbed the stepladder and, with strict instructions for me to hold the ladder steady, he proceeded to bore a hole in the ceiling. I began to chuckle.

"What's so funny?"

"The whole scenario," I replied, still chuckling. I was aware of the short, sturdy man in baggy old shorts, up a short, sturdy stepladder boring a hole in my bedroom ceiling and it suddenly appealed to my sense of humour. I felt that the hole was sure to be short and sturdy too. My humour was added to when the hole that the landlord had drilled seemed to form the pupil of an eye. The water stain had formed the rest of the huge "eye", which I knew would be looking down at me at nights.

"That oughta fix it," the landlord said cheerfully. "The dripping should stop in a minute. I'll paint over 'er when she dries."

"She" being the large eye on the ceiling.

"What if rainwater gets into the ceiling again?"

"You'll just have to keep the gutters clean of leaves," was the landlord's response.

"What about the problem of birds getting in the ceiling?"

"What about it?"

"Well, it's rather a worry."

"Don't you worry about it. They've got to nest somewhere," he replied. "Anyway, you're here to let them out."

I did not appreciate his woolly thinking. "What if a little bird gets in while I'm away for a week or so? The little thing would starve to death."

"I haven't found any dead birds up there in the ceiling."

"Yes, but it could happen!" I persisted. "Every time one gets inside, I have to go through the procedure of quietly putting the stool underneath the manhole cover, climbing up and lifting the cover to one side, then sitting on the sofa and reading or knitting or doing other handcrafts until the bird has the sense to come out. Then I have to gradually close the doors off until I can get the bird out through the French doors."

"Doesn't sound like too much of an effort to me."

"I have to ensure that no cats are around."

"That shouldn't be too difficult."

"No," I agreed. "Fortunately Katie is mostly over at the neighbours and Reilly out and about when a bird gets into the ceiling, but there will come a day when they're too quick for me and too quick for the bird."

"You'll just have to move a bit faster then, won't you?"

"*Please*...won't you do something? Some fairly fine netting put around the eaves should do the trick. It would also help keep most of the leaves out of the gutters."

"I suppose I could find something in my shed that would serve the purpose," he conceded grumpily.

I flashed him what I thought was a disarming and grateful smile. A gleam came into his eyes.

"Have you got a boyfriend?"

"No, and I'm not keen on having one either!" I tried to smile again, but quite frankly, I was getting rather fed up with the man.

Reilly sat on the bed and observed proceedings, his golden eyes rarely blinking. I wondered what he was thinking. It didn't take long to find out.

"You a good Christian woman and you have a man with a gleam in his eyes in your bedroom!"

"These circumstances are entirely different to what you're suggesting, Reilly!" I turned to see the landlord staring at me oddly.

"What did you say?"

"I was talking to Reilly," I said lamely. "I forget myself, sometimes."

"Oh, I talk to my cats all the time!"

It was nice to know the landlord was finally so understanding. I'm just glad he couldn't tune in to what Reilly was thinking. The big cat leaped off my bed, gave me an enigmatic look and walked out of the room.

A lady by the name of Roseanne Amberson once said that in the middle of a world that has always been a bit mad, the cat walks with confidence.

It did seem that way; even on the rare occasions when Reilly was in embarrassing situations, such as the time in Motueka when the neighbouring market gardener, fed up with cats digging up his seedlings, set a trap and when cats were caught inside the trap, the garden hose was turned on them.

Reilly was one of the cats caught, but was he fazed by the experience? Not at all; he came home wet but still with a dignified walk, and with his secret smile.

Ah yes, I knew the secret: he loved water, and neither he nor I ever let on to the market gardener that he was wasting his time trying to chase Reilly away. Indeed, as Theophile Gautier said: the cat is a dilettante in fur. Observing Reilly with that aloof air he so often adopted, I heartily agree.

***

# CHAPTER TEN

## *Don't Mess With The Big Bird*

It was a sunny Saturday, late morning. My washing was on the line, the birds were singing; scent from the flowers wafted on the light breeze and all was right with the world.

"I wanna go to the beach."

"What a good idea. Do you want to go right away?"

"When I make up my mind that I want to do something, it means *now!* You know, woman - *immediately!*"

"I get your drift, you chauvinistic cat. Maybe Katie would like to come too." I called her; she came piping and leaping over the fence from the neighbour's house.

"I'm here! I'm here!"

"How about a trip to the beach, Katie?"

"Ugh, no thank you; not today. I'm off back over the fence!"

"See?" Reilly looked smug. "I didn't think she'd want to come."

"Never mind that. I'll just lock up and off we'll go."

He chirruped around my legs and several times I almost fell over him as I tried to get out the door. Then we were off - it was far too nice a day to stay inside and the beach beckoned me every bit as it beckoned Reilly. As I didn't have a fireplace in the cottage, there was no need for me to collect driftwood as I'd needed to when I lived at the other address in Carter's Beach, and therefore there was no need for me to drive my car the short distance. Reilly ran in the kerbing.

"I fought them in the trenches, I fought dem on the beaches..."

"Who's "them", Reilly?"

"The enemy, of course!"

"Oh yes, I'd forgotten."

"Dat is a bad memory youse has got."

"Why does your language deteriorate every so often?"

"Whaddya mean deteriorate?"

"*That's* what I mean!"

Reilly muttered something as he ran. It sounded something like "I blame it all on me sad background, dat's what." A couple of the neighbours called out as we passed by.

"I see you've got your dog with you Amber!"

"He thinks he's one at times," I replied.

Reilly stopped for a few seconds and glared at me and then at the neighbours.

"I do *not!* How dare you all liken me to a dog! I am a *cat* - a most superior species!"

"Come on then, Grandiose One, and get going."

The neighbours looked at me, amusement written on their faces.

Reilly gave a growl and continued on his way, irritation showing in every line of his back. When we had reached the domain however, his irritation disappeared and up the big old pine tree he went, clawing his way up in a matter of seconds and peering at me from a sturdy branch.

"Can't see me!"

"Yes I can!" I called. "Your eyes are showing."

"Kids are like that once they get up into trees aren't they?" said a smiling matronly woman who was walking arm in arm with her husband.

"It's my cat up there," I said. It seemed that I often had to explain to people that it was not a kid up the tree, but a cat.

"Oh well, they can be like kids too, can't they?" She gave a weak smile.

If I've heard her phrase once, I've heard it a hundred times from others. I felt that I really should have a little recorder set up, a simple one to enable me to quickly press the play button every time I took my cats for a walk. It would save me having to repeat myself every time a woman made a comment on my "kids". I also wished that once, just once, Reilly would get up the tree when no one else was around.

When the couple started to walk away, Reilly scrambled down from the tree, chirruped and ran towards the beach.

"Oh look Elmer, there goes the pussycat, on his way to the beach! What an odd little pussycat!" I heard them chuckling and dared to look at them, to see them now observing *me* - but with a wary look.

I've seen *that* look many times over the years too; it dubs me an eccentric. However, I always maintain one should be true to oneself no matter what, and if others can't accept that, then they are the ones with a problem.

"Hurry up, you weird woman, you!"

"Me weird? Huh! What a cheek!" I exclaimed.

So much for my lofty thoughts just before!

At the beach Reilly did his usual - gamboling and leaping in the soft sand, chirruping with the sheer delight of being a happy, healthy cat in a place he so loved. Up and down the driftwood he went, scratching here, scratching there, doing swift turns while airborne. Dancing and prancing over and over, then rushing down to the water's edge where he went in for a paddle.

"Come on in Ma, the water's fine!"

I've heard those words before too of course, numerous times. I went for a paddle too, and enjoyed the bliss of the clean sea air, the cry of gulls overhead, and just generally reveled in the enjoyment of being alive in such a lovely place.

Reilly looked funny as he swam up and down and several little kiddies coming down to the water with their mother in tow pointed and shouted: "Mummy, Mummy, *look!* A pussycat having a swim! Mummy, what a *funny* pussy!"

The mother laughed at Reilly's antics and indeed, he showed off his great skill at swimming and cavorting in the water. The small children were enchanted and so was the mother, but she gave me several wary looks, despite my cheerful hello.

Presently they left and we were ready to move on too. Reilly shook himself like a dog when he strode out of the sea like a sort of "Cat God of the Ocean", and promptly sat on the wet sand to wash himself. It was a cursory wash only, as if to say, well that's that, then. Another day at the beach and in for a swim, ho hum.

And that kind of spoilt his stately exit from the sea.

When he began walking up the beach he made an amusing sight with wet sand clinging to his ample rear.

"I am the greatest!" he announced.

"Not with that wet sandy bottom, you're not!" I replied, smiling.

"A mere detail, woman!" he said haughtily and ran up the beach into the soft sand.

In the distance we heard a droning sound which developed into kind of chuffa chuffa noise. It sounded like a helicopter - and it was.

"Holy cow! Dat's one big bird! Dis is where discretion is the better part of valour!"

He shot up behind a large piece of driftwood. Three small late model cars traveled down the clean wet beach together, the helicopter flying close above them. It was quite exciting to watch and the action was repeated several times. I assumed correctly, as I discovered later, that the new cars were being filmed for a television advertisement.

Soon the helicopter and the cars did their last run and all turned back.

"Come on Reilly, the fun's over."

"Fun? You call dat *fun?* I'm not coming out yet where dat big bird can see me!"

"It's only a helicopter and you're quite safe."

Reluctantly he emerged from behind the drift log and walked slowly and warily with me, then stopped.

"I'm not going any further, woman!"

"Okay, I'll take you around the road and then we'll go home."

He mumbled in agreement. We walked through a gap between blackberry and gorse bushes and headed up the gravel road which skirted the Carter's Beach Domain. Many years before, the land which now formed the domain had been reclaimed from the sea and was gradually developed into a domain and camping area. Up the far end of the domain was an unusual looking caravan. As we neared it I realized that it was actually a film truck, with the helicopter parked next to it. The crew were standing just outside the open door to the truck and when Reilly and I passed by they all laughed.

"Hi!" I called out cheerily.

"Hi!" they called back, and one of them added: "we saw you and your cat at the beach. Some cat you've got there!"

I agreed and proudly walked onwards, after being told that they were there to shoot a car ad for television. I don't know who was preening the most, Reilly or me!

When we returned home, Katie was sitting outside the French door.

"Guess what I saw, Katie O'Brien!"

"Oh Reilly, I wasn't there, so I don't know!"

"Eat your heart out, small cat! I have just seen the biggest bird ever - it's called a helicopter bird!"

"I've never heard of it before."

"Well, you wouldn't, would you? If *I've* only just seen it, how could *you* possibly know anything about it?"

"You don't know *everything*, Reilly."

He assumed a cunning look which, even in his bedraggled state, did not seem to diminish him in any way.

"I know that you are a very beautiful cat, Katie O'Brien!"

"Oh Reilly, you can be so wonderful!"

And she pranced and preened around him in pussycat happiness.

"Credit given where it's due, I always say."

And he looked smugger than ever, if that was possible.

**

A lady by the name of May Wilkens said that cats love one so much - more than they will allow. But that they have so much wisdom they keep it to themselves. I'd often thought along those lines but decided to test the theory again, to see how much truth there was in May Wilkens' words.

Reilly was on my bed, lying on his back soaking up the sunshine that streamed through the window on this perfect, clear West Coast day. He opened one eye at my approach.

"Do you love me?" I asked, kneeling by the bed and not attempting to stroke him because Reilly had the wicked habit of appearing soft, beautiful and approachable but a swift bop with a paw, claws extended, told you that he was anything but soft.

"What sort of question is *that?*"

"A simple one, I would have thought."

"Why ask me? Don't you already know?"

"One doesn't always know with you, cat."

"I live here, don't I?"

"Yes you do, but I suspect that's because no one else would *have* you!"

"Oh I like that! I like that indeed! *Huh!*"

"That's nice, Reilly," I said, grinning. "I'm glad you do."

He rolled to one side and faced me with a decidedly wicked look in his great golden eyes.

"Haven't I sworn my devotion to you always?"

"No you have not! Look at the scratches on my arms!"

"Consider them trophies fit for a wonderful human," he replied, his eyes half shut. Was *he* being sarcastic? It was hard to tell; he yawned and appeared to be genuine and then I relaxed and thought: how wonderful! My cat *does* love me!

Reilly leaped off the bed, chirruped and left the room. I heard his distinctive snicker, but was this a double bluff? Hard to tell, but the warm glow within me told me I was accepting that his love for me was genuine. With a happy sigh I stood up and quietly walked out the door. Reilly was back with Katie, who'd been having a snooze on the crocheted rug on the sofa.

"I tell you, Katie O'Brien, we've got to keep our wits about us!"

"Why?"

"*Because,* small cat, if you let humans think you love them, it makes you vulnerable."

"What's wrong with that?"

"Keep 'em on their toes, dat's what I say! No pussy-footing around! We've had to claw *our* way through life - let dem rely on *us* for a change!"

"Oh Reilly, you are *so* funny!"

"O'Reilly, dat's me!" he preened, and snuggled into the blanket.

The day was warm, but there's something about a rumpled, crocheted wool blanket on a velvet fabric sofa that can make the meanest cat purr in pleasure and totally ignore the fact that a warm rug on a warm day would overheat them somewhat.

Reilly began purring and added: "Not only am I a naturally funny cat, but I display all the best attributes of a cat!"

I entered the room. "Oh *really,* Reilly!" I protested at his conceit.

"Really, O'Reilly! Oh, that's funny, Mum!" Katie piped.

Reilly growled at her. "Whose side are you on, anyway?"

Katie blinked at him owlishly with her big green eyes.

"I love you both," she said simply, and started washing him. Reilly forgot himself for a moment and shut his eyes in ecstasy, but when he suddenly realised that I was still standing there watching them he growled and pulled away from Katie.

"Arrrgh! Gerroff!"

"Never mind Katie dear," I said when I saw her hurt look. "He's only saying that because he knew I was watching."

"Go away, woman. I want to go back to sleep."

"Really?"

"Yes, really."

"Okay then," I said with a grin, and went to the fridge where I retrieved a can of whipped cream. I popped the top off and there was a sudden rush for the treat from both cats.

"Gimme, gimme!"

"Ooo, a treat for us, Mum!"

"Still tired, Reilly?" I gloated. "Never mind. I know you're far too weary for a dish of lovely whipped cream, so I'll give it to Katie."

"Gimme gimme!" he demanded, banging against my legs. Katie just looked up at me with her great jewel-like green eyes. She didn't need to say anything. I put some cream into her bowl and held Reilly back from stealing it. Reilly promptly changed tactics.

"Youse is a very beautiful mummy," he said in a wheedling tone.

"Groveling now, are we?"

"When it suits me. Who is a lovely girl, den?"

"Katie, I expect you mean."

"No, *you,* woman! Now, gimme some of dat cream!" He gave a gentle nudge on my legs this time and even a cursory lick on my hand as I bent down to squeeze the nozzle and let the cream flow forth.

I think Reilly won that round again, because as soon as he'd had enough, he chirruped, licked his whiskers - then took a flying leap back onto the sofa, to begin kneading the rug. His golden eyes were half shut again, giving him a rather sleazy appearance.

"Come on Katie O'Brien. I want some feminine company."

"Will I do instead?" I asked, smiling.

"Naw. I'll put up with Katie for a change."

Katie jumped up to join him. "Oh Reilly, you're wonderful!"

"Glad someone appreciates me!" he said with a leer, and promptly fell asleep.

I temporarily gave up. No matter what I did or said, Reilly always seemed to have the last word.

*Seemed* to have? No, he nearly *always* had the last word!

It reminded me of a time many years ago when we lived on a farm and my father said to us, "I always have the last word", and my sister Coralie cheekily commented, "What, 'yes, Mum?'"

Dad was not pleased at the comment, given the look he gave Coralie, who just laughed, and Mum looked very pleased at having scored points, albeit from an unexpected direction.

***

# CHAPTER ELEVEN

## *One-Upmanship*

A writer named Barbara Wester put it very succinctly: one reason why we admire cats is for their proficiency in one-upmanship. They always seem to come out on top, no matter what they are doing - or pretend they do.

Reilly appeared to be asleep, but I saw the light reflect off one half-closed golden eye. It was as if he was thinking: you think you've got me worked out, but if you think *that,* then you're in for a few shocks!

I say I *thought* he might be thinking that: usually I understood very well what he was thinking, but just to confound the issue, from time to time he would close off his thoughts to me.

It was just the look left on his face that would lead me to assume what he might be thinking.

"Never assume, woman!" he said suddenly, giving my heart a leap.

"Er...why?"

"Because it can make an ass out of you and me!"

"That's an old saying. *I* told you that in the first place!"

"Of course you did, woman." He waited until I appeared mollified then added: "and I'm just reiterating it."

**

There was no doubt that Reilly was easily able to keep me on my toes! On several more occasions while I was in the cottage, birds made their way into the ceiling and couldn't find their way out again, until I intervened. I spoke to the landlord again about it as my earlier pleadings hadn't proved as fruitful as I'd hoped.

"Why shouldn't the birds come inside? They've got to have *somewhere* to stay," he said yet again.

I thought his point of view was highly impractical and told him so. "What if they die there?" I persisted.

"Well, they haven't, have they?"

"Not as far as I know...but thanks to me so far," I said.

"They'll find their way out."

"But don't you see? They *didn't!* That's why I did what I did."

The landlord gave me a long-suffering look. "There needs to be ventilation under the roof," he said patiently.

I felt like stamping my foot. "I couldn't agree more. But could you possibly put a fairly fine mesh in the gaps so air can get in, but birds can't?"

"That's a lot of trouble to go to," he replied.

"What if I was away for a few days and a little bird or two got in and died of hunger? What if there was torrential rain and strong wind when I was away and the leaves built up in the gutters again and water got back into the ceiling and made the ceiling sag, causing expensive damage?"

"Okay, okay, you've made your point!"

It still took a while for the landlord to do the job and in the meantime I had several birds - blackbirds and starlings, find their way inside. I would go through my usual routine of ensuring the cats were outside, taking my stepstool to place it directly under the manhole cover, then stepping up onto the stool so I could reach the cover and quietly lift it to one side. Then I would enter the lounge and sit on the sofa and read or do handcrafts while waiting for the bird to literally see the light and make his or her way out. As soon as the bird flew into the lounge I would close the door to the tiny foyer area where the manhole cover was, and open the French doors and hope Reilly and Katie didn't come inside in the meantime.

On one occasion Reilly did, and it was a very panic-stricken bird which finally made it to freedom, albeit with a couple of feathers missing where Reilly had made a mighty leap and dislodged them en route.

I was amused at his expression.

"What are you smirking for?"

"*Smiling,* Reilly. I'm smiling at *you,* cat! You almost look embarrassed!"

"Yeah, well..." and without finishing what he was going to say, he sat to wash his paws. That seems to be a maxim for cats; when in doubt or when embarrassed, simply sit and wash your paws. Nonchalance will have us fooled every time...at least that's what *they* think. Of course it pays to let a cat *think* he has you fooled. Otherwise there could be an argument.

"Are you embarrassed?" I couldn't resist asking.

"Who, me? Of *course* not! What a silly thing to say! We cats are *never* embarrassed."

"Then why did you look that way?"

"Oh, maybe I expected to catch a little more of the bird than just a measly couple of feathers!" he said airily.

"I'm glad you didn't!" I exclaimed.

He appeared to shrug. If you don't think cats shrug, then look again sometime; shrugs are part and parcel of their nonchalant look!

"Then why the fuss? Why mention it at all?"

"Because I was curious, that's all."

"It's *our* job to be curious, not yours. It's your job to wait on me, hand and foot!"

"Or paw and paw," I grinned, "when *you* wait on *me!*"

Reilly glared, turned away and began washing himself - yes, and he shrugged again, I'd swear to it.

"God brought me into your life woman, and you should be grateful!"

"Oh I am, I am!" I said cheerfully. Reilly had just proven my theory of assuming nonchalance when embarrassed and another theory I'd had: of when embarrassed, push the guilt onto one's human, to save face. Not so very different from people, in fact.

"I prayed for a tough tomcat and I got you, a tough tom *kitten*, and I have never been disappointed," I said tenderly, bending over to stroke him in a rush of affection. He swiped at me, leaving his usual fine trail of blood. Irritated, I added: "except on an occasion such as this!"

"I'm still seeking revenge on humankind."

"Hmmm, 'Revenge is mine, sayeth the Lord'," I quoted.

"He wasn't talking about us cats - he was talking about people. They can never get things right, so God has to do it for them!"

"If we're going to have an argument about who is the superior species, you can forget it!" I snapped.

Reilly half-shut his eyes and gave me a knowing look.

"I rest my case!"

"I didn't know I was on trial," I retorted.

"Didn't you just say 'Vengeance is mine, sayeth the Lord'?"

"Of course I did - you heard me!"

"Well then, consider that scratch which you're now sucking at, *my* revenge! Since God created me, I have been given carte blanche to seek revenge whenever and wherever I can."

"What about wee Katie? She's had such a hard life but I've never heard *her* wanting to be vengeful."

"Katie is Katie and I am Seamus O'Reilly, Cat Extraordinaire."

"Yet again you said a mouthful," I said dryly, and went in search of Katie.

She was up the kowhai tree in the back yard.

"Hello, Mum! Such a lovely day!"

"Katie, you are a breath of fresh air!" I said with great feeling.

"Has Reilly been picking on you again?"

"You could say that," I said, looking down at the fresh new scratch on my hand. I still wear the scar from that scratch today, along with several others from Reilly.

"It's just as well that we can make some allowances for his chauvinism, isn't it, Mum?"

"Katie, when did you get to be such a wise little cat?"

"Oh, I was born that way...I just don't make a fuss about it."

There was no conceit there whatsoever. She was merely stating a fact.

I smiled. "You are a wise little cat indeed, Katie O'Brien."

Her big green eyes were like two rich jewels, framed by her dear little chocolate-coloured face.

"Ooo, thanks, Mum! But we do have to be wise around Reilly, don't we? It pays to let him think he rules the roost."

"But he already does, doesn't he?"

"No Mum...he only *thinks* he does!"

"We'll just have to go on letting him think he does, then."

"That's what I thought."

I heard snickering and turned to see Reilly disappearing around the corner.

"I suppose you heard all that?" I called.

"Never heard a word!" he called back.

I heard that distinctive snicker again.

\*\*\*

# CHAPTER TWELVE

## *A Doggy Rapport*

My friends Shelley and Kevin visited one Friday evening and as usual, brought their little dog Inky with them. Inky never seemed to walk, but had a way of prancing along on his tip-toes. His rich, deep chocolate brown coat gleamed in the overhead light.

I made a simple supper for us all and while we sat around talking, the animals began to entertain us.

Reilly sat on a chair and watched Inky and Katie circling each other, Inky excited at having a playmate and Katie quite unconcerned as she walked in a circle. Reilly looked amusing with his fluffy head low to the chair, his ear tufts sticking out more than usual and his big eyes gleaming. He appeared to be suppressing great mirth. I stared at him and he looked up briefly to stare back at me.

"Ho ho! This is *so* funny! The big brown rat circling my girlfriend!"

"So, you finally admit she's your girlfriend?"

"What?" said Kevin.

"Huh?" said Shelley.

"It's okay. I'm just talking to Reilly," I explained.

"You mad Irish washerwoman!" Shelley laughed. "It figures!"

Inky and Katie continued their circling until Katie became tired of it and wanted to lie down. Inky barked at her to get up and continue the game.

"Not now Inky...I want a rest."

"Come on, come on! I've been sleeping half the day and I want to play!"

Katie rolled onto her back and looked engagingly at Inky.

Reilly glared. "You *hussy!* You're not to do that to *anyone* but *me!*"

Katie's eyes were again shining like green jewels, and as she blinked slowly and began a sultry washing of herself, from the corner of my eye I saw Reilly rise up from his chair.

"Leave them alone Reilly," I warned. "They're only having fun."

"Dat's what worries me!"

Katie continued washing herself and when she'd had enough of Inky's pleas for her to play, she calmly got to her little paws and walked over to the drapes and hid behind them. Inky pounced on the shape she made and Katie swiped a paw through the drape at Inky. He barked in excitement and after a few minutes of this play, Katie walked out the side of the drape, leaving a rounded bump in the drape where she'd been. Inky gave her a brief look when she walked out, but continued to eyeball the hump in the drape.

"You daft dog, Inky!" Shelley exclaimed. Inky was still using his pointing instincts while Katie was back in her original place on the carpet, rolling and lolling around in extreme pleasure.

"Dat's my girl Katie," Reilly said. He jumped down to give her a quick wash, forgetting for a moment that we were all observing.

"You can be a nice cat when you want, Reilly," I remarked.

He leaped back, sat on his round little rump and gave me that nonchalant look.

"Who, me? If you think I was being soft with Katie, then think again!"

"I don't have to...and you don't have to play games with *me,* Seamus O'Reilly. I know you really like Katie."

Kevin and Shelley gave me bemused looks. They were used to me talking to Reilly as if he was a person. In many ways to me, he *is.* I could nearly always count on a stimulating conversation with him!

Inky gave up his close observation of the hump in the drape and turned to face the cats.

"How did you get out here, small cat?"

"You saw me walk out, big brown dog, and took no notice."

"Oh well I...er...ahem..." and Inky sat down, embarrassed.

Katie rolled around again and Reilly observed her with a jaundiced eye.

"Big brown dog? Fat brown rat, I say!"

"Oh Reilly, that's not nice!"

Katie rolled and squirmed some more.

"Nice, nice? Rhymes with spice! That's me! Full of zing and spice!"

"Tell me that you're full of sugar and spice and all things nice... tell me what you want to do..." Katie said, sing-song, and I was surprised. Much as I adored her, sometimes I had felt that she lacked enough spice of her own to stand up to Reilly.

He smirked. "You really want me to show you, babe?"

"I've suddenly changed my mind!"

She ran under the table and Reilly followed her, batting at her tail. Inky barked, keen to get in on this new game and Katie growled and hissed at Reilly who was swishing his tail, his eyes positively gleaming with mischief.

"This is more entertaining than the telly," laughed Shelley, who'd said similar things on other occasions when our pets were putting on an impromptu show for us. I agreed with her. Even the most entertaining comedy couldn't always match up to the amusement provided by Inky and my two cats.

**

Reilly and I were discussing the merits of dogs...or at least *I* was. Reilly was listening to me and putting his dollar's worth in every so often.

"They're not smart like us cats."

"Of course they're smart! Look at the St Bernard, or the German Shepherd...or any other breeds I could name."

"Don't bother naming them...I'm bored already."

"Intelligent species usually take an interest in everything," I pointed out.

"Thing, woman, *thing!* A dog is...indescribable."

"What about Gwyn? You used to have a lot of fun with her." Gwyn was the corgi who had lived next door when I lived at my previous Carter's Beach address.

"I liked to bait her, just to see her get mad. I can even take on several dogs at once!"

"That's what you do to *me* all the time."

"What? There's only *one* of you!"

"You know what I mean. You like to bait me, to try to get me mad."

"The only trouble is...I don't get you mad often enough, for my liking."

"Why you should even want to do such a thing beats me."

"Just as I've said time and time again, it's part of my revenge on the human species."

"Why bite the hand that feeds you?"

"How long is it since I've bitten you? Answer me that!"

"A wee while...maybe two days!"

"Yes, well...you should be grateful I let you go that long!"

"Sometimes you can be so nice; other times you are so *horrible.*"

He gave a smug look. "But you love me all the same!"

I nodded. "More fool me. How did we get around to this silly conversation?"

"It was already a silly one. You were talking about the merits... excuse me while I puke...of dogs."

"Go outside if that's what you're going to do!"

"It was a figure of speech, woman! Anyway, just to please you, what about a story on dogs?"

"What makes you think I have a story for you? Won't it make you sick?"

"You're always full of stories. Go on, get on with it. You might as well ruin my day properly!"

I folded my arms and glared at him. "Since you're being so jolly rude to me, I don't know that I should tell you anything!"

"BOYS, PLEASE! NOTHING PERSONAL...

...BUT YOUR MUMS REALLY ARE...!"

His eyes narrowed and then he rubbed against my legs. "Aw, go on, there's a nice girl."

I couldn't help the grin spreading over my face. Lord forgive me for being such a sucker! "Okay...here's a story about a dog. I can't remember her name so we'll call her Jess...actually, now that I've said that, I think her name really *was* Jess..."

"Yeah yeah, yeah yeah...get on with it, woman!"

"Anyway, I was having a really bad morning. One guy had just been to see me and talked almost non-stop about politics for about two hours...and then a phone call came from a guy who had to be one of the most ponderous people you could imagine. I discovered that the two men disliked each other, so at least I was able to get rid of one before the other arrived."

"Why did you even let the second one come, if he was going to be so boring?"

"It was part of my job as a journalist...you have to take the good with the bad, and all that..."

"Why?"

"Stop interrupting! Just as I said...you have to take the good with the bad. Anyway, guy number one left and guy number two arrived, all ready to settle in for another long chat about politics and the police department and one thing and another. I was beginning to feel my energy absolutely drain away."

"Why didn't you give him the old heave-ho?"

"Because I was a freelance journalist then, as I still am now and you have to take what work comes along, even if it is a crashing bore to write and the people leave you feeling like a zombie."

"Okay, get on with it, woman."

"I would, only you keep interrupting me, as usual. Anyway, as I was saying...the second guy droned on and on and finally it came time for him to leave. I was *thinking thank God! He's heading for the door! Quick Amber, get him out while he's that close!* So I got the door open and out he went and just as I was starting to breathe easier, the guy stopped and turned around... "oh, there's just one more thing I forgot to tell you..." and on he went for another quarter of an hour, out the front of my flat. I kept counting to ten, and said I'd better be going, that I had an appointment straight after lunch...but some people just can't take a hint, can they?"

Reilly sat and washed his paws. "No, they cannot," he agreed, and waited for my next torrent of words.

"Then he made a move again and I began to breathe easier... he took a couple of steps towards the gate and stopped and turned again. "Oh yes, I also forgot to tell you about..." and on he went again. It took half an hour for him to get to my front gate, and just as he turned for the third time to tell me something else..."

"What's all this got to do with a dog story?"

"Wait your patience, cat. I'm coming to that bit. Just as he turned for the third time, something caught his eye..."

"Ha ha! Your fist, probably!"

"I'm not like that, although there have been a few occasions when it was all I could do to restrain myself! No, the something that caught his eye was the neighbour's dog - a Rhodesian Ridgeback/ Boxer cross bitch, and she was wearing a pair of pants, with big bold flowers on them. "My God, I've never seen anything like *that* before!" said the man. Nor have I, I said, my spirits rising. The big dog looked so funny and she cheered me up enormously. She also looked at us as if to say: 'so what? I *always* wear this sort of garb? And isn't it *trendy!*'"

"What was she doing wearing pants, for God's sake?"

"She was in season."

"Summer or spring?"

"Don't be smart, cat. You know what I mean...she was on heat."

"Ugh, how disgusting!"

"I bet you don't think so when there's a lovely little girl cat around who's also in season!"

He gave me an arch look and carried on washing as if I'd said nothing at all that was bordering on sex. His look continued, and then his eyes narrowed and I was sure that he was suddenly remembering his little operation. Still, as I have mentioned in the past *that* little operation doesn't put off cats from doing what Nature dictates!

"So what's the moral of this long-winded story?"

"That, no matter how boring or uncomfortable your circumstances, there is always something just around the corner to lighten it."

Reilly got to his paws and stretched and yawned. "Took you long enough to say it, didn't it?"

Then he walked away with a snicker and I felt my temper rising. He turned and observed me, giving me an unfathomable look. I watched as the mischief took over and he positively smirked as he observed me, my hands on my hips and (probably) eyes glittering.

"My God, you're beautiful when you're angry!"

And with a chirrup he vanished into the bedroom and snickered when he heard the light thump of one of their toys hitting the wall.

"Temper, temper! Katie, I wouldn't go out there if I were you! The woman is throwing a paddy!"

"What about another story?" I called, my brief annoyance with Reilly swiftly waning.

"Is it safe to come out?"

"Of course it is."

Out they both came, scampering and leaping onto the sofa.

"On with the new story, den."

Okay, here goes. This one is about a dear little bird."

"Yummy, yummy," Reilly chortled.

"Don't be awful, Reilly. I was living in Nelson and was unhappy. I went into my bedroom and saw a little finch on my window sill. I went to the window and the small bird seemed unafraid. So I quietly opened the window and reached around to pick him up."

"Maybe it had flown into the glass and was stunned," Reilly said.

"I thought so too, but the finch was too alert and happy for me to pick him up. I brought him inside and talked quietly to him while he just sat there in my hand."

"Brave bird," Reilly commented. Katie said nothing; she just looked at Reilly through half-closed eyes and purred.

"Anyway, the little bird just carried on sitting there and after about ten minutes or so I took him back to the window and let him out. He sat on the sill for a few seconds, glanced back at me and then was off and away."

"What do you think he was there for?"

"I've read often since that time, that when people are sad and lonely, an animal, bird or butterfly is sent to that person to lift their spirits. It happened to me twice when I was in Martin Place, before you came on the scene, Reilly."

"So now you don't need any other animals or birds, coz now you have me! Reilly the Wondrous!"

"And me!" piped little Katie.

I smiled in agreement.

\*\*\*

# CHAPTER THIRTEEN

## *Mirror, Mirror On The Wall*

A new day dawned: the cats and I had slept well for a change. Reilly began his day with a wide yawn and a stretch. I watched the muscles ripple throughout his body and secretly marveled at his perfection. It was difficult to imagine that this magnificent cat was found by my friends - barely able to stand, and so dirty he was first thought to be a black kitten. What glorious shades of grey his fur had become and what a pure white on his face and tummy, a perfect foil for the varying shades of grey.

"You're watching me, woman."

"I know I am...just observing afresh."

He leaped onto my dressing table and stared in the mirror, his tail hanging hilariously over the front of the dresser.

"I'm so good-looking!" he said, turning his head this way and that.

"Conceited too," I remarked.

For an answer he gave a bored yawn and continued turning his head this way and that, presumably to check to see which side gave his best profile.

"Which is your best side for photographing?" I asked, laughing.

"I can't make up my mind," he conceded. "I think both profiles are equally handsome!"

I gave a derisive snort which woke up Katie. She saw Reilly sitting on my dresser.

"Why are you staring into Mum's mirror?"

"What does it look like? So I can see myself in all my glory, you silly little cat."

"Mum! He's being awful to me again!"

"Never mind Katie...it's the male ego. We've got to keep reminding him how magnificent he looks, otherwise he might forget and actually become a nice, normal cat."

"I am *above* normal. I have many attributes that other cats don't have!" he growled.

"At least I got a bite out of you!"

"Why try? I can give you a bite any time you like."

"Smart-mouthed cat." But I laughed anyway and Reilly continued with his preening as if I hadn't spoken. Then he suddenly squashed his nose up against the mirror.

"Oh!" I exclaimed. "Mirror, mirror on the wall, who is the fairest one of all?"

Reilly pulled his head back a few centimetres.

"*Handsome* is the word, woman! You're supposed to say mirror mirror on the wall, who is the most *handsome* one of all?"

"Since you're the only male in the house there's no choice - we'd have to say *you.*"

"Of course," he replied smugly, and then squashed his nose against the mirror again.

"What are you doing?"

"I'm squashing my nose. What does it *look* like?"

"It looks squashed, since you asked. But why *are* you doing it?"

"Because I feel like it."

"Why?"

"Does there have to be a reason? Whither the wind bloweth, woman, there bloweth I."

"Okay, windbag. Have it your way."

He ignored me and stared into the mirror again. Katie observed him, blinking her huge green eyes in astonishment at his conceit.

"I would love you more if you weren't so arrogant, Reilly."

"Who cares? I love me enough for both of us!"

"You said a big mouthful, Reilly."

"That's what your mumsy-wumsy often says."

He stuck his nose to the mirror again and left little marks. I was suddenly put in mind of a story I'd heard not long after I had moved to the West Coast. A final performance was held at the old Theatre Royal before it was due to be demolished. Following the performance there was a party, which is the usual procedure after theatre performances, but this one was particularly poignant - due to the pending closure of the old theatre.

One of the actors, a very overweight and outgoing fellow imbibed far more than he should have and felt the call of nature. He left the party for a few minutes to go to the toilet. He sat on the old porcelain lavatory and there was a resounding *crack!* as the old loo gave up under the pressure of age and enormous weight.

The actor collapsed along with the loo, cutting his ample rear end. He didn't feel much pain due to the amount of alcohol he'd drunk, but was mindful of the blood oozing from the cut.

"Damn!" he said in his drunken state. "I must put a plaster on that when I get home."

He pulled up his trousers with a "she'll be right, mate" attitude as often is the way with Kiwis, and back to the party he went, the cut throbbing only a little.

The party went on until the not-so-wee small hours and finally the fat actor went home. When he tried to remove his undies prior to crawling into bed he wondered why they were stuck to him. Then he remembered the oozing cut.

"Oh yeah - that's right, I cut me bum," he said to himself. "Better stick a plaster on it!" He took his undies off and the cut began bleeding again. He fetched some sticking plaster and, backing his huge moon of a behind up to the mirror, he stuck the plaster to the cut. "There, that should fix me bum!"

The next morning when the fat actor awoke he moved in his bed and discovered that the lower sheet was stuck to him.

"Musta lost me plaster," he said out loud. He searched the bed and couldn't find it, even when he pulled the sheets back. There was blood spotted in various places over the sheet where he had turned over in his sleep. Initially puzzled over the disappearance of his piece of sticking plaster, he shrugged his shoulders, yawned and went to the mirror to see what ravages to his face had been caused by partying so late.

He stopped short when he espied his plaster stuck to the mirror. Light dawned: he was so drunk he'd stuck the plaster to the mirrored *image* of his rear.

"It's a bum rap!" he'd said hilariously - that's the sort of man he was: large and hilarious, and he always enjoyed a good joke, even if it was against himself.

I told Reilly and Katie the story.

"Who would be so stupid as to put plaster on his reflection in the mirror?"

"He was drunk and it's very funny."

"The story should go like this: mirror mirror on the wall, who is the most wondrous cat of all?" he said, ignoring my last statement.

"I can imagine *you* doing that, Reilly."

That got his attention.

"What?"

"Getting drunk."

"I don't drink, except out of the loo," he said loftily. Which made a mockery of his words.

"Anyway, I thought of you when I told that story."

"Humph! Are you saying I've got a fat rear?" He glared at me in the mirror.

"Not at all, my dear cat. You reminded me of it when you stuck your nose to the mirror."

That made Reilly turn around.

"It's nice to see your face again, Reilly," Katie said, blinking again.

"I think so too," he said smugly.

"I may remind you again of the fat actor and the sticking plaster," I warned.

"I don't care. It's a funny story!"

"I didn't think you liked it."

"Well you thought wrong, so there!"

"Seamus O'Reilly, you're a twister."

"Yes Reilly, you are too!" piped Katie.

He glared at her. "Who asked *you?*"

"I'm just agreeing with Mum."

Reilly leaped off the dresser to the bed and approached Katie in attack-mode.

"But I do agree you're a most handsome cat," she added winningly, rolling over onto her back and arching her head over to gaze at him.

Reilly was mollified and sat back on his haunches while I, still sitting in bed, observed Katie in a new light. She could be quite a hussy when it suited her. She usually hid it well, under that exterior of innocence and always being eager to please.

Was *Reilly* ever eager to please? I don't recall him *ever* being that way, unless he cunningly hid it under some other guise. He gave Katie a quick wash and held her down with a strong paw when she began to squirm.

"Oh Reilly, you are so *masterful!*"

"O'Reilly, dat's me!"

He suddenly stopped washing her, aware I was watching in pleasure. He looked pointedly at the wall as if to distract me into thinking there was something unutterably fascinating about the plain wallpaper. I was not fooled, and I said so.

"I will not be distracted, Reilly!" I said firmly.

"Soooo, there's more to you dan all dat honey blonde hair!"

"Reilly, how dare you! If I've heard one remark about blondes, I've heard hundreds more. You really are the limit!"

Reilly smirked, his golden eyes glowing. "But I distracted you, did I not?"

"Oh...yes you did!" I threw a soft pillow at him. He ducked and leaped nimbly off the bed to claw his way around the outside of the bed base. Then off out the bedroom he went, chirruping happily.

"Reilly's such a naughty boy this morning, Mum," Katie piped. "But don't you just *love* him?"

I sighed. "Yes Katie I sure do, and he knows it. That's why he loves to give me such a hard time."

"It's not fair, is it Mum?"

"No Katie, it is *not* fair. Come on wee girl, it's time to get up." I climbed out of bed and for a moment I stared at the splotches Reilly had left on the mirror and thought of the fat actor, all those years ago.

Katie walked gracefully into the lounge where Reilly pounced on her.

"Eek! Mum! Reilly's picking on me again!"

I sped into the lounge and Reilly disappeared with a snigger into one of my pot cupboards and clattered around in there.

"Come on Katie. Let's see how mad we can make the woman!"

"Why?" little Katie piped.

"Just because I feel like it, dat's why."

"You are such a mean cat sometimes, Reilly. No, I'm not coming in."

He ignored her last statement, clattered and banged around some more and dodged out of my way when I tried to remove him.

"I *like* to be mean! Ha ha, you can't catch me!"

"Can't I just?" I said grimly. "We shall see about *that!*"

He carried on thumping around in the pot cupboard and when he had stopped for a breather, I opened the fridge door and took out the pressurized can of whipped cream. I took the lid off: it made an interesting *thwock* sound, as always. Reilly was out in a flash.

"Gimme gimme."

"Okay pussycats, you can have some each." I squirted cream into each of their bowls and watched with enormous pleasure when they sat side by side, furiously licking up the cream. When Reilly had almost finished I quickly picked him up, laid him against my shoulder and stroked him. He leaned further into my shoulder and began a deep, rumbling purr, just as he did in the past when I'd put on some nice music and would dance slowly around the room with him. Still holding him, I turned on the stereo and the song "Loyal" by New Zealand's Dave Dobbyn began to play.

"Loyal, yeah dat's me, woman."

"Reilly, I didn't think you cared!" His claws sunk into me. "Ouch!"

"Dat's for dat remark. Of *course* I care! It's just un-catly of me to go all mushy and say it."

"But Katie tells me often."

"She's a girl."

"What's that got to do with it?"

"Soppy, that's what females are."

"Yet, here you are, sinking into my shoulder and purring with pleasure because you have a tummy full of cream and a nice song playing on the stereo," I reminded him. "And anyway, I *did* catch you! You thought I couldn't."

"I'll ignore that remark. Just don't get carried away with this lovey-dovey business. Now, put me down, woman! I haven't even finished my first course of breakfast. What are you trying to do, *starve* a poor cat?"

"Oh sure you look starved!" I said waspishly. "Remember the story I just told you about the fat actor?"

"No way could I ever be likened to a fat actor."

"Carry on eating the way you do and I may have to re-name you! You could become Reilly the Huge, or Reilly the Blimp, instead of Reilly the Magnificent, or simply Fat Cat."

"Seamus O'Reilly does very nicely, thank you," he said loftily as I put him down. He walked back to his bowl with an injured air.

"Have I hurt your feelings?" I said, astonished, and bent to stroke him. Like a flash he swiped at me. *"Ow!"*

"That's for hurting my feelings."

"I didn't think you had any," I said sourly, as I licked the faint trail of blood off my wrist. He walked away from his now-empty bowl and replied with a snigger.

"I'll have the rest of my breakfast whenever you're ready, my good woman."

And that was that, I thought.

As usual, Reilly had scored again.

***

# CHAPTER FOURTEEN

## *Pussycat Showers And Shopping*

Later that same day, after I'd completed my assignments for the various nation-wide, South Island-wide and local publications, I went outside to relax for a while before heading to the bathroom for a shower. Both cats were outside on the patio watching a few ants with intense interest. A light breeze rippled their fur: what wonderful shades of grey and deep chocolate brown, to reveal the smoke effect of near-white fur underneath. I marveled again at their creation, and their absorption in the tiny ants that were attracted to a miniscule piece of meat - dropped there by a passing seagull, perhaps.

Katie moved in closer and attempted to lick at the fragment of meat then, as ants began to crawl over her dainty nose, she snuffled and snorted to brush them off.

"Silly cat. I could have told you about ants."

"Why didn't you?"

"Couldn't be bothered. Besides, you learn better if you find out for yourself. That's the best education in the world."

I was amused at my cats - so opposite in nature and both so perfect in their creation; Reilly's glorious golden eyes and Katie's brilliant green ones - gazing at each other in understanding. It was a poignant moment, lost only when Katie brushed a paw across her nose and walked inside, Reilly quietly following. I sat on the sofa and watched Katie. Reilly plodded into my bedroom for a short nap. This is the poem I wrote while observing Katie in all her seemingly innocent ways.

### Katie O'Brien

Dark and dreamy
with a golden heart
Katie O'Brien observes
with kindred feeling;
her great green eyes
compassionate, filled with love
and comfort and ease
for those who weep.

Body sweetly perfumed
with earth's dainty wildflowers
and heavenly boronia,
she tiptoes into the room
and gladdens the heart and soul
with her figure, small and perfect:
a full measure of her given love, shared love
is her continued, life-long goal.

\*\*

She inspected her food bowl. It was empty and I wasn't intending to fill it again just yet, knowing how both cats have a penchant for gluttony. She jumped onto the dining table and when I told her to get down, she just gazed at me innocently and beautifully until I was compelled to rise from the sofa and pick her off the table for a cuddle. I suspected that it was her ploy for an extra cuddle.

"You do that just so I'll pick you up, don't you Katie?" I said into her ultra-soft fur. She drooled with pleasure and kneaded against my shoulder.

"Sometimes," she admitted, dribbling a little. "I can't seem to help myself." She rubbed up against my cheek and purred contentedly. "Do you mind, Mum?"

How could I, after *that?*

"Of course not, Katie." After a few minutes I put her onto the sofa and headed to the bathroom for a shower. As soon as I undressed and stepped in, both cats stepped in too. "You daft things!" I exclaimed.

Reilly looked up at me with a leer.

"I remember you saying to me at that other place we lived in up the road from here - come on in, the water's fine, you said. So now we're *both* taking you up on your invitation!"

"Yes, but that was just about a *year* ago."

"I took it as a standing order, thank you very much, and I'm accepting on behalf of myself and Katie, isn't that right, Katie?"

"Oooh, yes, please!"

"You're supposed to say something more assertive than that!"

"Like what?"

"Er...something like: move over, we're a-coming in!"

"Okay...move over Mum, we're a-coming in!"

"You're already in I see, you daft things." I reached over to close the bathroom door so they couldn't get back out of the tiny room and take their sodden bodies to the sofa or my bed. After a short frolic they'd had enough and one by one they stepped out of the shower box and shook themselves - over the clean clothes I'd forgotten that I'd put on the floor.

Too late, they also added very wet paw prints to my clothes, meaning I'd have to decide on something else to wear.

"Ta very much for walking over my clothes, cats!" I said coolly.

"Did you put a sign up saying: 'Keep off the clothes'? No, you did *not!*"

"Can you actually read too, clever cat?"

"If I know about signs, I can *read!* Cats can do *anything.*"

"It's supposed to be...girls can do anything," I said, rushing through the rest of my shower.

119

"Stuff and nonsense," said Reilly, and Katie looked at him in a way I had never seen her look at him before. It was as if she was about to stick up for the rights of the females of all species, but thought it prudent not to say anything - at least not yet. Maybe because she was hardly at her best - soaking wet and attempting to lick herself dry. She looked so thin and tiny with her wet fur that she reminded me of the day when I had first brought her home from the animal shelter.

When I stepped out of the shower I quickly rubbed both cats down; Katie accepted the rubbing with pleasure but Reilly barely tolerated it.

"Ergh! Gerroff, woman!"

"I'm not having you drip all over my furniture."

"Put some clothes on. You look disgraceful!"

"I will when I'm good and ready. Avert your eyes cat, if you don't like the look of me."

"You've got big bumps."

"You are a rude cat! These are my womanly curves..."

"Curves, *curves!* Good gracious woman, you'd sink the Titanic!"

"It's already sunk - a long time ago," I retorted.

"Were you on it then? For shame!"

"Get out right now, cat!" I opened the door and off they both scampered into the lounge. I went to my bedroom to get dressed. By the time I emerged, fully dressed, Katie was sitting on the sofa, cuddled into my crocheted rug and Reilly was on the floor, chewing sheaths off his claws.

"I've told you about that before, Reilly. If you must do that, do it outside, otherwise I really *will* paint your claws pink!"

"You and whose army?" he sneered.

"I'll wait until you're asleep."

"I'll know, woman - if you so much as put one drop of pink nail varnish on my claws I shall have my revenge."

"How, this time?" I asked, standing in front of him with my arms folded across my chest in a mutinous stance.

"Maybe I'll take my revenge in another way - maybe I'll pick on Katie! Grrr!"

"You wouldn't!"

"Wouldn't I?" His eyes gleamed. "Watch me - Katie, come here!"

"Eek! Go away you awful cat! Mum, make him go away."

"Yes Reilly, outside you go, if you're going to be in that sort of mood." I picked him up in a firm hold and walked towards the French doors. He reached out and stuck claws into one of the drapes and pulled threads. It took another minute to extricate his claws and then I set him down outside.

"Killjoy! I was about to have some fun!"

"Find some fun elsewhere for a change, and leave wee Katie alone. She hasn't done you any harm."

"That's beside the point. I'm in a mood and have lots of energy to spare!"

"Go for a run around the block. Go and chase stray dogs or something. In fact, that's a very good idea - I could put you to work with the Buller District Council! You could work in the Animal Control Department, rounding up stray dogs!"

"Huh! How much would they pay me?"

"I'd make sure you were on full wages," I replied, grinning.

He gave me a superior look. "You get dafter every day, woman."

"It's you who's making me that way!" I called as he ran away sniggering, to shoot up the eucalyptus tree at the front of my rental property.

**

One morning soon afterwards, my beekeeper friend Gary came to visit me, to collect some eucalyptus nuts off the big tree to give to a friend of his for a planting program. I was working on a couple of articles at the time, but I welcomed the break. It was always good to see Gary. He has to be the most relaxed, easy-going man I have ever met, and always has a store of anecdotes to pass on.

Gary lived two houses away from the Carter's Beach shop and I would often see him when I was out for a walk with one or both of the cats. He always seemed amused to see me with my cats milling around my legs.

"Out for a walk with your children today I see," he'd say with a cheerful grin.

"Yeah, out to let them off for a run...and myself too," I'd reply.

One particular day I went to the shop and told Reilly to stay outside. Katie had decided to stay home on this cool, breezy day. Reilly sat by the door just like a well-behaved dog would - but only for about two minutes. There were things in the shop he wanted to have a look at, and new people to inspect. He rushed in and prowled around. I hoped I'd have my few groceries bought before the owner and his assistant noticed Reilly being very nosy.

Gary entered the shop and espied Reilly.

"Kids can't stay home, huh?" he laughed.

A little girl who'd just entered the shop with her mother saw fluffy Reilly and squeaked: "Mummy, mummy, look at the pussy! He's here to do his shopping!"

I thought that was very amusing and so did Gary and the child's mother, but the owner and his assistant were not so amused.

"Get that cat out of here! It's against regulations!" snapped the owner.

"Tell that to Reilly," I retorted. "He would go where angels fear to tread."

This amused Gary even more, which added to the shop owner's annoyance.

"Scat - shoo!" the shop owner said loudly.

"Grrr - how *dare* you treat a prospective customer like that?" Reilly hissed.

"Poor pussy is not allowed in here, Mummy," said the little girl.

"No, poor pussy," echoed her sweet little mother.

"Yes," Gary added, "poor little pussycat! Never mind, maybe you didn't have the brand of pet food he likes anyway!"

Enraged, the owner's eyes flashed dangerously and his assistant added to the melee.

"Out! Out!" she yelled. Reilly growled and managed to slip under the counter so he could inspect what was behind it.

"Grrr, what horrible shoes you're wearing! Ugh! Not even *I* would bite *dem* feet! Boring, *boring!*"

"Out of here!" shouted the owner.

"Scat, cat!" said the assistant.

"Grrr, hiss to you too. I don't like your shop anyway!"

Out he shot from underneath the counter and ran outside, hissing and growling.

"Poor little pussycat," said the little girl again.

"Yes, poor wee thing," said her mother.

"I don't want to come into this shop any more, Mummy."

"I don't think I do either," the mother said grimly and gave the owner a gimlet look. The thought assailed me: *and therein lies another pussycat with claws, under the sweet exterior - thank you, little lady!*

She marched out, her tiny daughter following: two dear little champions for the cause of pussycats.

I tried not to laugh as I handed my money over for my purchases. "Just as long as you don't charge me double for your lost custom," I said with a tiny smile. Gary laughed out loud and the shop owner glared at us both.

"You probably sent that cat in here on purpose," he grumped. I smiled and left, Gary following. Out of earshot of the owner and his assistant I told Gary that I had a good mind to send Reilly back into the shop, just for the hell of it. We had a jolly good chuckle over the incident and went our separate ways.

Reilly was waiting for me just around the corner.

"I shall never darken the door of that man's shop again."

"That's probably what he's hoping for," I laughed.

\*\*\*

# CHAPTER FIFTEEN

## *Cats In A Hot Sports Car*

It was time to go to Nelson again, to catch up with my family and friends. I phoned my friend Lou in Nelson to see if I could stay with her and she readily said yes. My next call was to Lois at the Waimangaroa Cattery. She said yes too and so, with things falling nicely into place I packed a bag ready for the next day and finalised a few articles ready for posting away. The cats were agitated: they knew something was going on.

"Are we going for a ride in the car?" asked Reilly.

"Oooh, I don't like cars!" said Katie, her eyes more enormous than ever.

"I know you don't, but we *are* going in the car. I'll have a little something for you Katie, to help you relax."

"A whiskey and tonic should do the trick!" Reilly sneered.

"Maybe I should give you something to help you relax too," I said sternly.

"Don't *need* it," he replied airily and scampered away to leap onto the table and down again, then up on the bench and down again from there too.

"Are we going to Aunty Lou's house? Oh joy!"

"No, you and Katie are not. You're going to Aunty Lois' house for a few days."

"Oh all right. I like Aunty Lois too."

125

Soon after, I gave Katie a tranquilizer and about three-quarters of an hour after that I set off for the tiny settlement of Waimangaroa, which was twenty-three kilometres away.

"Go faster, woman! This *is* a sports car, isn't it?"

"Of course it is, but I don't want to break the speed limit."

"Come, come, I don't believe you."

"Too bad Reilly. Now...be quiet, you're upsetting Katie."

"Doesn't take much to upset her."

"Nasty cat, Reilly."

"Sissy cat."

"Mum, make him stop!"

"Cut it out, Reilly!" I said loudly.

For once, he remained quiet for at least several minutes, except for the occasional snigger - but I didn't dare ask him what he was thinking. I was afraid of his answer.

When we arrived at the cattery I stayed to talk to Lois for a while.

"How do the two of them get on?" she asked, gesturing to my cats who were now in a big roomy cage, checking out the new smells.

"Oh you know Reilly, he can be a bully, but when he thinks no-one's watching, he can be really sweet to Katie."

Lois laughed. "That sounds like Reilly all over."

Katie was still very wobbly so Lois took her in to the sleeping room and put her in a smaller, padded cage so she could sleep off the effects of the tranquilizer.

"I wished I didn't have to use those things, but she gets in such a state when I don't use them," I sighed. "In that respect I wish she was more like Reilly. He can't *wait* to get in the car."

"Not many cats *are* like Reilly," Lois observed, and I agreed.

\*\*

It was a pleasant trip to Nelson, as always. On the way I kept a look-out for interesting events and sights in case I could write an article about them and take photographs. That was one of the disadvantages of being a freelancer. It didn't matter where you

126

went or what you did, you always had to be on the look-out for another prospective story. As most of my work was in the rural field, so to speak, this meant limitations. I did not write hard news stories for instance, having no interest in that type of writing. My leanings were towards feature stories, of almost any length.

In Murchison, roughly halfway between Westport and Nelson, I interviewed a fascinating elderly man who took me to a pretty area to the west of the township where an old stationary engine had been parked up for many years. Long grass grew up and around the old engine, adding to its nostalgic air and general fascination for me. The nice man had a wonderful memory and as I have an interest in machinery and a deep love of historical objects there was plenty to talk about. I took photographs of the man standing next to his early 1900s stationary engine and they were published along with the story in a couple of nationwide magazines.

Even after many years as a journalist, the novelty of seeing my work in print dimmed only when I wasn't pleased with the layout, or there were cuts in the text due to extra advertising having come in to the publication at the last minute. Still, it was nice to know my work was going nationwide and when I went overseas I was able to do interviews and photography which would further the scope of my work. Doing interviews via interpreter was sometimes tough going, but I always felt a real sense of achievement when the job was done.

A German girl I once interviewed in Westport had been living there for many years and had the biggest collection of cat memorabilia I'd ever seen. Cats that meowed (real cats of course, as well as figurines with "meow" mechanisms), slept and played in pewter, silver, crystal, porcelain, clay, wood or whatever; Roswitha had collected them from all over the world. Her collection was even larger than my friend Lou's, although Lou's included some very rare figurines indeed.

The feature story I wrote about Roswitha and her cat collection also went nationwide and that story too, gave me a real sense of achievement.

I reached Nelson, visiting family members on the outskirts of the city, then drove on to Lou's and her husband Dave's elegant home on a hill overlooking one of the suburbs and out to sea. The view is magnificent and at night it's like a fairyland, as most cities are at night.

"What are you writing about now?" Lou asked. "More dairy effluent and the many uses for it?"

"No," I grinned. "Today's topics are old stationary engines, petrol-fueled and used back in the early 1900s for driving a sawmill."

"You lucky pig!" she said dryly.

"Aren't I just?" I laughed. But I meant it, as I always loved writing about old stationary engines of any model.

I've always enjoyed Lou's bracing humour: it kept one on one's toes and I always returned to the Coast feeling amused and rejuvenated. Her animals too, always welcomed me as their Aunty Amber. Indeed it was and is a real pleasure to be with other people who totally understand cats.

**

As always when I traveled to Nelson, I would visit family members as well as try to get other leads on articles to write.

Family visits over and chores completed, I said goodbye and thanked Lou and Dave for having me to stay, and I set off on my journey back to the Coast, calling in to see my mother one more time on the way. Nearly three hours after leaving my mother's flat in Richmond, I arrived in Westport and headed back northwards towards Waimangaroa on the West Coast. Many times I had wished I could have taken a shorter cut, but the lie of the land did not allow for that.

The cats were fine, although from the little Lois said, I gained the impression that Reilly had started getting into mischief.

"He keeps looking sideways at my chooks," she said.

"Don't trust him an inch," I advised her. "Your chooks may be almost his size, but as he thinks nothing of taking on dogs many times his size, your dear little hens would be no match for him."

Lois nodded in agreement. "I'd already figured that out." Her Red Shaver hens clucked around outside their pen and pecked happily at the grass.

Reilly went rigid in my arms at the sight of them.

"Get those ideas out of your head," I told him sternly. "Just as well we've got your cage here."

"Don't cage me in, woman. I like to be as free as the air."

"I know - that's what worries me."

Lois glanced curiously at me and when I said I was replying to Reilly's thoughts, she nodded understandingly. It gives me such a warm rush of feeling when I know people understand me!

We put the cats in the car; the seat belts went around the cages just nicely.

"I *hate* being in this little cage! How would *you* like being stuck in a cage like this?"

"And have *you* drive the car? What a laugh! You'd never reach the pedals! Imagine if a reporter saw you driving my car - what a field day that reporter would have!"

"*You're* a reporter, so...report!"

I thought some rather angry thoughts but kept them to myself as I paid Lois, thanked her and waved goodbye as I set off back to Carter's Beach. Maybe I should have left the cats until the next day, before heading back up to Waimangaroa to pick them up. *Too late now,* I sighed as I drove and listened to the cats chattering in their cages. I had already told Lois about what time I expected to be back, and that I would telephone her if I was going to stay another day. That didn't happen and the trip had gone as planned. Katie was nicely tranquilized for the trip home and apart from her chattering with Reilly, our journey back was uneventful.

The first thing I did on stopping up my driveway was to let the cats out of their cages. They stretched and yawned and stretched some more. It was lovely to see them again, but Reilly looked ripe for mischief. He was. He swiped at Katie who backed off, fortunately not as unsteadily as I would have expected, given that her tranquilizer would not have worn off.

"What did you do *that* for?" I asked sternly.

129

"Just because I felt like it. Do I have to explain everything I do?"

"No," I sighed. "I guess not. You're just being your usual, unreasonable self!"

"Huh! I like *that!* I thought it was very reasonable of me to agree to go to Aunty Lois' place, when I really wanted to go to Nelson."

"You had no choice in the matter. Anyway, I didn't think you'd ever want to go up that way again."

"Why not?"

"That's where you came from - that part of the island. Lucky for Lou and her son Shane that you were rescued!"

"Maybe I wanted to thank them," Reilly said slyly, his eyes half shut.

"I doubt it. You kept picking on Tess when you lived there."

"Who's Tess?"

"Their dog. I thought you cats remembered everything - or do you have selective memory?"

"Maybe - I can't remember!" he said succinctly before he gave Katie another bop and leaped away chirruping, to scamper up the eucalyptus tree.

"He's such a beast Mum, but I do adore him," Katie said as she rubbed around my legs. I was pleased to see she had almost recovered from the effects of the tranquilizer.

"I know you do Katie - so do I, and Reilly knows it. That's why he gets away with so much." I bent to stroke her and rub her ears. "You're precious too, Katie," I added softly. She replied by purring loudly and dribbling with pleasure. What a dear little cat - so eager to please and so grateful for any attention.

I unpacked the car and drove it into the garage while the cats expended some of their excess energy by chasing each other up and down the eucalyptus tree. I called them for their dinner and down the tree they rocketed, barely pausing to stop at the open French door and both skidded on the vinyl flooring in the tiny kitchen area. I laughed and Reilly looked at me mournfully.

"We might have been *hurt!*"

"Nonsense!" I replied briskly. "You're as tough as old boots!"

He growled and stuck his head into his food bowl. Katie hadn't wasted any time; her bowl was already half-empty and she was keeping an eye on Reilly's bowl. He was aware of her sidelong glances.

"Keep yer cotton-pickin' paws off my food, small cat."

"You said nothing about my mouth...so..."

And she cheekily made a quick snatch at a chunky piece of beef.

"Huh! Just a minute here, small feline! Just you remember where you came from!"

"I'm remembering and that's why I'm still snatching food where I can."

"Remember your waistline....you could end up being a fat, waddling pussycat. Who would love you den?"

"My Mum still would, even if you didn't!"

I observed them, grinning, and enjoyed their repartee. It was a nice change to see Katie sticking up for herself for a change.

Reilly harumphed and to my great amusement, used a paw to push his bowl further away from Katie's. There was silence for a few more minutes as they concentrated on their food.

Katie looked up from her empty bowl.

"Anyway Reilly, what about where *you* came from? You could hardly stand up when you were found, you were that weak!"

"That's totally beside the point, Katie O'Brien. I was talking about *you,* not me."

With that he made a grand exit, moving soundlessly, but I'd swear I heard him snigger while waiting for me to open the French door for him so he could resume his play.

***

# CHAPTER SIXTEEN

## *The Call Of The Sea*

The next day the cats still had a surplus of energy due to their confinement at the cattery, so I decided to take them both for a walk to the beach. The weather didn't look too promising but I figured we could make it to the beach and back before it began to rain.

"How about a walk to the beach, cats?"

"Thought you'd never ask," said Reilly.

"Ooo, yes please!" said Katie.

After locking the cottage, off we went, much to the amusement of some of the neighbours.

"You should have made your kids take their raincoats!" a buxom lady called out.

"Pink ones to match yours!" called her husband.

I laughed. "Reilly would *hate* that. He loathes pink."

"How do you know?"

"He told me," I replied smoothly and gave a wave as we walked on. I felt the exchange of amused glances, but wasn't worried. After all, it had happened too many times before and anyway it was a nice day - even with rain threatening.

"How dare that man suggest I wear a pink raincoat?"

"You could have a pink raincoat to match your pink claws - that's when you let me paint them!" I chortled.

Reilly ran off down the kerbing in a huff, while Katie stayed with me.

"*I* like pink, Mum."

"I know you do, dear. Come on, we have to catch up with Reilly. He's in a snotty mood with me."

"He's an egotistical bully."

"Sure, but if you tell him that, he'll only preen further."

We caught up with him two corners away, when he'd stopped to out-glare a big ginger tomcat.

"Who do you think you are, O Grey One?" said the big ginger cat.

"I'm sometimes known as the Caped One, or the Caped Cat."

"Why Caped Cat?" asked Ginger, momentarily diverted.

"Because sometimes I wear a cape, dat's why, stoopid!" Reilly said in an alley-cat drawl.

"Who are you calling stupid?"

"You, stoopid."

"This is *my* territory!"

"Yeah, and I'm gonna take it over!"

"You and whose army?"

"Don't need an army. Me - I'm general, major and sergeant all rolled into one!"

"That must be why you're so fat!"

"Am not!"

"Are too, fat grey one."

"Watch it buster - you get no second chances!"

"Hiss, hiss!"

"Snarl!"

"Oh come *on*, Reilly! Leave that poor cat alone!"

Reilly glared at the ginger cat again and then sat on his haunches to begin washing his face.

"Now dat I think of it, I don't want yer territory anyway, ginger one."

"What's wrong with it?" said Ginger, diverted again.

"I've decided it's not good enough for a cat such as me!"

With that, he chirruped and ran off ahead of us.

133

"Never mind pussycat," I said to Ginger. "He does this sort of thing all the time. You have a very *nice* territory." I bent to stroke him and gradually his ruffled fur settled down and he began to purr.

"Thanks lady," he said, and walked back over his territory, mollified.

Off down the domain we all headed. As expected, Reilly shot up the pine tree and peered down at us from the branches.

"Think I'll stay up here for a while."

"You wanted to go to the beach."

"So I did."

With that, he chirruped and leaped down and, still chirruping, ran across the domain to the beach. It made a nice change that there was no couple nearby to ask me about my little boy up the tree.

Katie meowed piteously.

"Stay with me Katie, if you're nervous."

"Oh I am! There could be big dogs down there!"

"Reilly will chase them off for you."

"Will he really?"

"Of course he will. There are few things he likes better than to chase dogs...and the bigger, the better!"

"That's all right then."

She ran ahead happily and caught up with Reilly when he stopped to investigate some strange scents. He batted at her when she affectionately pushed into his side, and gave her a quick wash. When he saw me watching he put his head in the air, pretending that he hadn't shown any affection to Katie at all and pranced off, his tail arched and swishing to one side in the sheer joy of being outside in the fresh, moisture-laden air. The rain looked suspiciously close, but being used to torrential downpours, if it rained a little while we were out, it didn't matter at all.

Down the lane the cats ran, pausing every minute to sniff at a gorse bush here, a scrubby broom bush there, and then raise their heads to sniff at the salty breeze. It was intoxicating and

I thought afresh of the simple joy of going for a walk in pretty surroundings.

Since the cats' energy was still on the excessive side I decided to walk along the beach in the other direction - towards the rising plumes of steam and smoke from the cement works at Cape Foulwind. The clean curve of beach and the distant plumes would have been a graphic artist's delight I thought, as we walked slowly along the wet sand. Ten minutes later we came across the small creek which had curved a rut into the sand and had changed its course slightly, from when I'd last been up that end of the beach.

We followed the course of the creek away from the sea and clambered over ancient drift logs which had been there for so long, intermingling with other flotsam and jetsam that they were beginning to rot, and hardy salt-resistant plants sprang from them in bold green clumps, giving them new life.

*Like Phoenix rising from the ashes* I thought, and was greatly amused when Reilly, who had temporarily disappeared over the back of a log, suddenly rose up majestically in front of Katie and said *"Boo!"*

Katie leaped upwards in fright.

"Another sort of Phoenix rising from the ashes, you two," I said out loud and both cats this time gave me a look as if I had gone bonkers.

The slight trail which ran adjacent to the creek meandered for part of the way into pasture land which had two paddocks linked by a narrow gravel road. I noticed some old, weather-beaten fabric which looked like part of an old sheet draped over fencing, which was in about the same condition. It reminded me of the time not so long before when I was on-call for the Westport News and one of my jobs was to telephone the person in charge at the Suter Art Gallery in Nelson and ask questions about the winning exhibits of the most recent big arts competition. There had been a few West Coast competitors, one of whom was placed as a winner in his particular section.

I asked the lady in charge about the overall winner and what the exhibit was called.

"Er...I can't quite remember but it had a fancy sort of title," she said hesitantly.

"What did it look like?" I persisted.

"Well...you know, one of those modern art things - I don't always understand them - it kind of looks like soiled bed linen stuck in a frame with a few bits of other stuff hanging from it."

"Maybe it *was* soiled bed linen! Was it described as innovating?" I added cynically.

"I do believe it was!" she said, quite brightly this time. "How did you know?"

"You could call it a lucky guess," I said dryly, having already read that word many times before as a description for various winners of art competitions.

At least she'd been honest in how she had viewed the winning entry. I wondered to what lengths so-called modern art would be taken before someone finally shouted "enough is enough!"

That incident in turn, reminded me of a humorous little story about two art collectors who were discussing the disadvantages of modern art. "I'm not going into that exhibition," one collector said, gesturing towards a sign for one. "The last time I went to one of those modern art exhibitions I accidentally wound up buying the art gallery stair banister!"

Odd how I could suddenly be clearly transported back to the telephone conversation with the lady from the art gallery (although I guess the lady risked her job if she'd been overheard describing the "innovating" winning entry as "soiled bed linen"!) and then the humorous little story, by the sight of that fragment of old sheeting stuck to an even older fence with grass growing up and around it. To my way of thinking, it far better represented art than the arts competition winning entry.

"Oh good, a piece of old stuff to rip at!" said Reilly, completely ruining my wayward train of thought as he raked his claws down the fabric and instantly turned it into tatty old ribbons.

"You can't leave *anything* alone, can you Reilly?" said Katie, who for once observed him disdainfully. Usually she looked at him in hero-worship.

"Now *that* is what I call real art!" Reilly responded, looking from me to the tatty ribbons of fabric lifting in the salty breeze. I wondered if he could read my thoughts.

"Of *course* I can! Am I not one of God's perfect, innovative creations? Isn't that how we often converse? And didn't you more or less tell those people that you answered my thoughts?"

That sure answered my musings! I grinned and nodded, then looked at the sky when I felt a few drops of rain.

"Can we go back to the beach? I wanna go for a swim!"

"I don't think so Reilly. It's starting to rain. Why, you might get *wet!*" I laughed.

"Not as wet as I would if I went into the sea!"

"Possibly not, but it's too far to trek back down there and we've still got quite a way to go through here, yet."

Reilly snorted in displeasure but I'm sure that even he could see the sense of what I was saying. The temperature dropped a little and the sky grew darker. I knew we would have to hurry back home before the heavens opened. Sometimes the rain is so heavy on the Coast it seems unbelievable, and electrical storms in this part of the world are spectacular and very humbling indeed by their display.

I wrote this poem that evening in memory of the storm following.

### Two Lights

Perfumed candle
butterfly-flickering
in the dimmed room: frightened
cat's eyes, round
and gleaming
in the soft rosy light
from the slender candle.

137

\*

Harsh, spectacular blues
from the lightning
awakening black rain-washed skies,
punctuated by the
presence of Thor
riding the night in his
chariots of war.

\*

Two lights, inside and out:
one to light the skies
in all its surreal majesty
and the other - small perhaps,
but of hope and faith....

each an enhancement
of itself
in its own particular way.

\*\*

We moved quickly through gorse and broom to the road which used to flank the sea shore many years before, prior to the land being reclaimed. We walked past old cottages that once looked out over the sea but hadn't done so for many decades, not since the domain was formed from the old sea beach and a gentle stop bank built to help withstand the occasional unexpected king tides which, when aided by fierce winds and heavy rain, would try to claim back land that once belonged to the sea. It is a magical place, and one to which I return several times a year.

Around the corner we went, then around another two corners and we were home and back inside - just before the big drops of rain came, followed by lightning and deep rumbles of thunder. Reilly's frightened eyes were reflected for a second as lightning lit up the room, followed by more thunder. Reilly shot under the bed, flattening his body and splaying his legs out in an amusing fashion to enable the tight fit. Thunder was one of the few things that frightened him, and it wasn't until he had heard a great clap of thunder one afternoon some months before that Reilly discovered he could, after all, fit under my new bed with its lower base.

Katie surprisingly, did not seem too disturbed by the thunder and happily sat by me when the sky darkened even further as evening approached and clouds became an even deeper shade of grey. The rain bucketed down; the neighbours' nikau palms seemed to lash back at the high winds and rain. And then the sky was beautifully lit up - almost like day. Katie and I watched in awe.

"Gee Mum, we could have been out in that!"

"I'm sure glad we aren't," I said fervently, but was glad all the same of our pleasant walk to the beach and up through the paddocks. It was a real refreshing of the spirit and a day I will never forget.

\*\*\*

# CHAPTER SEVENTEEN

## *Male Domination*

The storm over, many of the neighbours' trees had a forlorn look and I couldn't help but wonder about the bird population and I said so.

"Ha! Saves me having to catch dem on the wing, if dey're already dead!"

"How can you be so horrible and unfeeling, Reilly?"

"Easy, dat's life!"

He was right and if I thought nature was cruel at times, it's God who in His great wisdom designed the storms to break and prune and launder; to refresh and renew. Who of us have not marveled at the clarity of a new day after there has been rain in the night, and have not enjoyed the rain-washed sweet air?

Reilly was fully recovered after his ordeal with the terrific thunder and lightning the evening before and indeed, even *he* seemed rain-washed. It crossed my mind I could have written brain-washed but as he's looking at me with a very jaundiced eye, I shall pretend I haven't written that. There are times when discretion is far more prudent than boldness will ever be!

"Gimme some paper, woman! I want something to rip and tear at!"

"Then I'd better get you some real quick - can't have you tearing up the furniture."

He stopped for a scratch then he rolled over and over on the carpet, to lie upside down under the coffee table. He did look funny. When he saw me grinning he proceeded to pull the magazines from the rack just above his head and tear the covers off.

"Too slow, woman! I have to get my own paper!"

Katie sat nearby observing, her big green eyes widening further at his antics.

"You're so amusing, Reilly!"

"I know! And not only am I funny, but I am *tough* and *mean!* Grrr!"

He chewed at the magazines, spitting out bits of the pages in a sloppy mess onto the floor.

"Yuk! I hate the taste of glossy paper! Gimme some newspaper!"

I screwed up some newspaper into makeshift balls and tossed them to him. He happily held one of them between his paws and tore at it with his fangs, spitting out bits. I was amused to read on one of the sodden pieces "...is the ideal food for your cat."

I dared not try to grab the magazines which were next to him in a mess; Reilly was like lightning with his claws - fast, furious and effective. He leaped out from under the coffee table in one fluid movement and dashed into the bedroom to claw his way around the outside of my mattress base then, when I ran in to admonish him, he flattened himself to crawl underneath and turn over on his back to claw his way across the other side - where Katie was waiting to tell him off too.

"Reilly, you are a *dreadful* cat!"

"Yup, dat's me! A dreadful, adorable cat!" He took a swipe at Katie and missed her by a millimetre. Not caring that he'd missed making a connection with his paw, he swiveled around under the bed and clawed his way back to the other side.

I knew how to get him out. All I had to do was go to the fridge and get out the can of cream and pop the lid off. It worked again but I cunningly had also got out the can of flea spray and had quietly opened the back door. When Reilly shot into the kitchen area I grabbed him by his scruff, got him outside and applied flea spray.

"Get that thing away - arrgh! If you've gotta spray me, spray me wid the cream outa da can! I will never trust another human being as long as I live!"

"I've heard all that before," I said, putting the can down to ruffle his fur for better application of the spray. With a sudden jerk he broke away from me and dashed off to sit on the back lawn and glare at me while he scratched.

"You can't do both at the same time!" I called.

"Can't I just! Watch me, woman."

He proceeded to have a jolly good scratch as the spray took effect, then he'd stop for a few seconds to glare at me, and begin scratching again. Katie was nowhere to be seen, but I figured I'd catch her for spraying when she least expected it. But every time I sprayed *her,* she would gaze at me so sadly with those huge green eyes, that I loathed spraying her. She made me feel so guilty.

Reilly came bounding towards me.

"Get out of my way! Dis is my territory and I am an angry cat!"

"You're so dominant Reilly. Why can't you be nice for a change?"

He snorted. "Coz nice gets sickening and boring after a while."

I leaned against the kowhai tree and folded my arms. "Let me tell you a little story about another cat I once had."

"*Once* had! What did you do with him or her? Overdose the cat on flea spray application?"

"Don't be silly Reilly - let me get a word in, will you?"

He stuck a paw over his face in a long-suffering fashion. "Ye Gods! Oh *no!* If a woman says 'let me get a word in' - *no, no, no!* One word stretches to ten, and a hundred, then a zillion - you could be there for *hours!"*

"You'd give any chatterbox woman a run for her money," I observed dryly.

"Knitting, recipes and tatting! Babies, baby food, kindy and such! *Gross!"*

"I wasn't going to tell you about any of those sort of things, but I'll have you know they are good and decent things in life. God told us to embrace all the things in life which are good and decent!"

142

"On and on and on...I *knew* it! Look, get this other story over before I cat-a-poult myself to your legs and scratch dem!"

"It would only be the hundredth time you would have done that," I said coolly, not to be outdone. All the same, I adopted a more wary pose just in case Reilly did carry out his threat. "I had this cat - a female, whom I called Rafferty..." I began, and Reilly interrupted.

"*Rafferty!* For a girl cat?"

"Don't interrupt. She suited the name and she was tough like you - *is* tough still, for all I know. This man I know who has a very dictatorial way with women..."

"Did he dictate to you?" Reilly interrupted again.

"He tried," I answered, "but he didn't get very far."

Reilly stared at my face and sat back on his haunches.

"Sometimes there's a steeliness in you which surprises me, woman."

"Just you remember that when you get a bit too smart with me," I said, my eyes narrowing.

"On with the story!"

I sighed. "Yes...well, anyway one day this man, who knew what a tough little cat Rafferty could be, picked her up and said: 'now listen here Rafferty - it's about time you were put under control!' She looked up at him for about two seconds then quickly raked a claw across his face. 'Ow!' he yelled. 'She's drawn blood! How *dare* she do that to me!' I said to him: I have, several times warned you that she had a mind of her own!"

"So, what's the moral of dis story?"

"You mustn't try to dominate, that's what!" I retorted.

"Some of you females enjoy it though," Reilly said slyly.

"Some, not all," I conceded.

"So, where did Rafferty go to?"

"She went to live in a lovely home north of here, with trees in the big back yard. I was going to Australia to live and it would have been too much for the cats to all go over there and be in quarantine for many weeks as well."

143

"So you farmed your cats out while you went gallivanting off to Australia! Charming!"

"I'd hardly say it was *charming*, cat! I had the 'flu when I went; the job I'd gone over there for had gone to someone else by the time I had got there and other job prospects were not good."

"Never mind woman. Look on the bright side - you weren't bitten by a poisonous snake or spider or eaten by a crocodile and you came back fit and well."

"How do you know all that?"

"Easy. It wasn't a croc, since you're still here on dis planet, and nor was it a poisonous snake or spider, for the same reason and anyway I'm the Grey One and Caped Cat all rolled into one. I'm the one who knows all and sees all and what's more, I have thousands of years of knowledge and discernment behind me."

"You're a know-it-all, is that what you're saying?"

"Just call me Sage, babe!"

He walked off sniggering. I hate it - I really *hate* it when he has the last word, so I thought I would outdo him for once.

"Sage is a kind of herb, so perhaps I should call you Herb, or better still, Herbert?"

But there was no answer from Reilly although I am more than certain that he'd heard me, even though he was deemed to be out of earshot.

So maybe he simply decided that my comment wasn't worth a reply.

**

It was a mellow evening weeks later. Spring had arrived with seemingly little change in the weather, but clumps of daffodils growing at random in paddocks were a sure sign that soon lambs would be gamboling among the daffodils. The sight reminded me of a book I had to review once, and I was not happy about being asked to do the task. The book, written by a man who was deeply depressed over his mother's death, poured out his anger against God, using many biblical passages out of context. I had ended the review with the words: "after all, who can watch a lamb in springtime, gamboling among the daffodils at random in lush green grass and say there is no God?"

As was the usual procedure, I sent a copy of the review along with an accompanying letter to the man concerned, who was still so angry at God and so angry with my review that he sent pages and pages of a computer printout of reasons not to believe in God's promises. It made me sad for the man, who had once been a preacher and when his mother had died, had turned his back on God. I was told by a fellow journalist at the local newspaper office that the man's reaction was most likely due to the fact that his mother waited on him hand and foot and when she was no longer there to do so, the man couldn't cope and was furious with his mother to have the audacity to up and die. I had agreed at the time that that was a distinct possibility.

"Why the glum face?" said Reilly, snuggling up to me as I sat in the French doorway, looking out over the front lawn.

"I was thinking about a very sad, very angry man," I replied, stroking Reilly. He purred in pleasure and once again it struck me how adorable Reilly could be when it suited him. It suited him this evening to be nice to me.

"He can't forgive, huh?"

"No," I agreed. "He cannot. Most of all, I get the feeling he's blaming God for his own guilt, in some way. His mother must have been expected to wait on him, hand and foot."

"Humans always blame God...even the insurance companies do it. I hear they won't pay out on things they call an act of God."

"Times have changed a bit since then, fortunately, but you still hear the saying."

"No wonder God designed creatures such as us, to give you poor, misguided human beings some stability in your lives!"

"*Stability?*" I said sternly. "My life has been turned upside down since you came on the scene, cat!"

"Yeah, but look at yer now. If dat ain't roses in yer cheeks woman, I dunno what dey are!"

I laughed and Reilly looked smug.

"Now that *you're* sorted out, I think I'll sort out dat little female cat who lives here."

"You mean Katie O'Brien," I said smoothly.

"Oh is *dat* her name? I almost forgot!"

"What, the most evolved of animals - *forgot?* She's your girlfriend, isn't she?"

"We're friends only," he said succinctly, and gave me that superior look I know so well.

"Katie probably thinks differently," I said, secretly admiring him with his glorious winter coat still intact.

"Yeah well, she's a girl, isn't she? It's common knowledge that girls think differently!"

"Viva la difference!" I joked, but meant it all the same.

"Where is she, anyway?"

"Sleeping on my bed."

"Sleeping, on so fine an evening. Scandalous! A tragedy! I'll soon sort *dis* out!"

With a chirrup, he did an about-turn and ran into the bedroom. Within seconds I heard: "Reilly you are a pest at times, but I so *adore* you!"

"How could you possibly do anything else but adore me?" was his lofty reply. "It's lucky for you females that you have *me* here!"

"Ooo, yes indeed! Mum's a lucky human and I am a lucky little cat!"

Was there a hint of sarcasm in my little Katie? Surely not! But if there was, it seemed like Reilly's ways were catching.

***

# CHAPTER EIGHTEEN

## *It's That Man Again*

I was really busy again. That was the way of freelancing; a feast or a famine, although having said that, most of the time my writing work had been pretty stable, but every so often there was a lull in the amount of writing work available. Or maybe it was simply that I worked so hard and when I had caught up with all my stories, it seemed as if the work had run out.

Despite always being on the lookout for story ideas, I was aware that it was time for my kitties to have their annual vaccinations. I thought about it for a day or so, but decided that there was no time like the present, and anyway, as there was a lull in my work, it was a good time to get this unpleasant task out of the way.

"We have to take a little trip," I told my cats when they came running inside, just after I had made a phone call to the vet.

Reilly looked at me suspiciously and Katie turned her big green eyes on me.

"Does this mean we're going to Nelson to see Aunty Lou, or up to see our nice Aunty Lois at Waimangaroa?" Katie wanted to know.

"No, not yet. This little trip is for your own good."

"Oh yeah?" Reilly growled. "Whenever I hear dem words: 'dis is for your own good' I am already on high alert!"

"Being on high alert is not a bad thing, although one should relax from time to time otherwise one will get awfully stressed out," I said, smiling.

"Is dat so? Why don't you tell us straight den, where are we going?"

"To the vet." There was no other way around telling them.

"Oh yeah? What for? So he can stick dat glass thingy up my rear?"

"Well now, that would be a part of it," I said carefully.

"You mean, dere's more dan dat?"

I noticed that Reilly's speech was deteriorating again.

"Yes there is, but this treatment will stop you both contracting any nasties."

"Nasties? Nasty dogs and nasty cats like dat Misty next door?"

"No, I meant nasty diseases."

"So what's the man in the long white coat going to do? Take us away to the funny farm?"

"No, you will receive a vaccination that prevents the nasty diseases. You've had the vaccination before."

"When's this going to happen?"

"Fairly soon," I told them both. Katie said nothing, but looked mournful. They sure knew how to make me feel bad, but I knew this was a job that simply had to be done. What I did *not* tell them was that the job was going to be done that afternoon. Had I told them, you can bet your boots that my cats would disappear for the day and would most likely stay away until early into the evening, coming home only when they knew the vet surgery was closed for the day.

**

I acted casually all through lunchtime and even stayed in very casual gear to help reduce their suspicion. It was a lovely day and I decided that a trip to the beach was in order.

"How about we go for a wee drive and then go to the beach?" I suggested, looking out the window to observe soft fluffy clouds scudding across the sky. I could see that rain would be well on the way by later on that afternoon, and so time was of the essence, as the saying goes.

"I CAN BE NICE — BUT I'M NOT GOING TO BE!"

"Yeah! Why not! But why aren't we walking, as we usually do?" Reilly stared at me, his suspicions eased, but not totally gone.

"Have a look at the sky, cat. You see those clouds? They're telling me that we'll have rain later on this afternoon."

"You mean that you talk to the clouds? Woman, you're even dafter than I first thought!" Reilly sniggered.

I didn't mind that he sniggered. In fact, I didn't mind if he kept up his sniggering for quite a while. At least it helped to keep his suspicions at bay.

Katie wasn't too keen on getting in the car but when Reilly nudged into her flank just before I put her in her cage and told her what a lovely girl she was, she soon settled down. I had a cage in the car for Reilly as well, just in case.

"A shame dat you have to put her in a cage every time we go out in da car, woman!" he said shortly. "Luckily I happen to love going out in the car. No cages for me, unless it's a long trip then... sigh, I have to go in a cage."

"You know Katie, she's not a tough, all-seeing, all-knowing cat like you," I said easily.

Reilly half-closed his eyes as he sat on the seat, and then closed one eye completely. "Hmmm...are you being smart?"

"No, just stating a fact," I said. "It's true Reilly; you really are a remarkable cat."

"Glad to know you appreciate that fact," he replied. "Now, off we go, woman!"

Off we went, my first stop being at the vet's surgery. I parked in the parking area reserved for people and their pets, and quickly got out, opened the door on the passenger side and lifted up Reilly. He went rigid in my arms.

"Where are we going first? I thought we were going to the beach?"

"And so we are, but first I want you to meet someone."

"Who?"

"It's a surprise," I said, for want of something better to tell him.

Luckily the waiting room was empty and the smiling, round-faced young vet nurse said I was able to go straight into the vet's consulting room where the warm-hearted vet was, standing there waiting for us. He was the same one who had given Reilly his "little operation" some time back, but I hoped Reilly had forgotten.

"Hello Reilly," the vet said as he gave the stainless steel table top a wipe down. "We meet again!"

"We do?" Reilly said.

For a few seconds it seemed as if Reilly had forgotten, and I was glad. All the same, it had been a long time since we'd been there and so much had happened in our lives in the meantime.

The vet turned his back and was busy for a moment with something in a small cupboard. I was pretty sure he was retrieving the necessary vaccination and other materials, and was staying quiet about it.

"I don't like the smell in here!" Reilly yowled, wriggling to get down. I held him firm, however.

"Don't worry Reilly, it's only a quick visit here and then I'll take you back to the car and bring Katie in so she can meet this nice man."

The vet turned and looked at me strangely. It was the same look he'd given me when I had told him on the day of Reilly's operation that I believed Reilly's birth date to be around the seventeenth of March - St Patrick's Day, and the vet had agreed with me.

He quickly but gently lifted Reilly's tail and inserted a thermometer.

"Get that thing outa my rear!" he shouted, wriggling. But the vet was well used to animals struggling to get away from the indignity of having a foreign body stuck up their rears, and chatted quietly about the weather while waiting for the result.

"Weather? How would you like a dose of heavy rain? Namely, me peeing all over the front of your fancy white coat?"

"Now, now Reilly, that's not nice," I said, and again the vet looked strangely at me.

I really don't know why he looked strangely at me. After all, I thought, vets should be well used to pet owners talking to their animals, and picking up on the animals' thoughts and feelings. In Reilly's case, he was wont to making his feelings very clear!

The vet turned away and returned with a slender syringe. Reilly took one look and wriggled out of my arms and stood on his hind legs, glaring at the vet.

"I thought you were supposed to be a nice man, but now you're going to stick me with a needle! How *dare* you! I can be nice, but I'm not going to be, so there!"

But the vet wasn't too concerned, despite Reilly's glaring and hissing. Without further ado he grabbed Reilly by his scruff and deftly inserted the needle, rubbing the area gently afterwards.

"See? That wasn't so bad now was it?" He said to Reilly, who sat back on the table, growling a little, but was much happier now that the deed was done. "No nasty flu's and whatnot now, big fellow. You certainly are a big handsome fellow, aren't you?"

Reilly preened. "If you say so, but I do happen to agree with you!"

"Reilly's agreeing with you," I said with a smile.

"Amazing isn't it, how animals' owners seem to know what their pet is thinking!"

"That's so true," I agreed.

The vet knew I had another cat to bring in and that I would pay as soon as Katie too had been inoculated. With a nod and smile of understanding he gestured for me to precede him out the door.

"Goodbye Reilly," The vet called as he went to the counter and the vet nurse held the door open for me. "See you again in due course!"

"Not if I see you first!" Reilly said, and proceeded to wash a paw while still in my arms, as if nothing much has transpired at all. Golly, he was so *good* at that!

I took Reilly outside to my car, opened the passenger door and Reilly leaped up to the back ledge where he sat happily, surveying the parking area with great interest. He had no interest in getting into his cage, which was not surprising. I quickly took the seatbelt from around Katie's cage and lifted the cage out and closed the door, ensuring first that the window was down a little to let fresh air in. I didn't see any point in locking the door, since Reilly was now inside the car. At times he was better than any watchdog!

In we went, into the waiting room. The nurse took one look at Katie and exclaimed over her.

"Oh what a dear little cat!" she said. "She looks like a toy!"

"Katie is Reilly's girlfriend," I said, smiling.

"I bet he just adores her," the nurse said.

"He does, but doesn't like people to know it!"

"I understand completely," she said, and I knew she really did. "The vet is ready for Katie now." She gestured for me to return to the consulting room, and I carried Katie in. Her eyes were huge and round.

The vet lifted her from her cage and, grinning broadly said: "a lot smaller than your other puss."

"Yes she is. She's Reilly's girlfriend," I repeated. The vet gave me an arch look, which I expected.

"Now young lady," he said as he lifted her tail and carefully and expertly inserted the thermometer, "here we go." Again he chatted about the weather for a moment or two while Katie's eyes looked even larger.

"It smells so strange in here Mum," she chattered.

"I know Katie, but isn't it lovely and clean!"

Katie chattered some more as the vet removed the thermometer and inspected it. "All normal, same as Reilly's. Good to see." He swiftly fetched a new syringe and inoculated her. "There you go young Katie. All done for another year."

Katie didn't even have time to let out a peep of protest.

Soon, after having paid for both cats' vaccinations, we were back in the car and on our way to the beach. Neither cat appeared to have any side effects from the vaccinations, but I did think it would be a good idea to keep our visit to the beach shorter than usual, so they both could have a good rest afterwards.

"How are you feeling, Katie?" I asked anyway, just as we rounded the corner before heading onto the last straight stretch of road before entering Carter's Beach.

"Fine thanks Mum," she replied, chattering away quite happily. It seemed a little strange to me, given that she normally hated being in the car. Yet Reilly often *demanded* to be taken out for a drive in the car.

We reached the beach and Reilly was out in a flash, chirruping happily as he sped down the beach, to race up onto a big old drift log and sharpen his claws. It was the same drift log that he always first sped up to. His ears back, and purring loudly, he ripped into that big old log and tiny bits of the rotting wood flew off in all directions. I let Katie out of her cage and she went down the beach at a considerably more sedate pace, and joined Reilly on the driftwood, where they appeared to be deep in conversation.

Shortly afterwards they both went for a scamper up the beach. The temperature had dropped quickly and the scudding clouds were more plentiful and had grown darker. It wasn't long before I felt the first few drops of rain.

The cats came racing up to me.

"Let's go home, woman! It's starting to rain!"

I needed no second bidding. We all quickly returned to the car and Reilly leaped in as soon as I had opened the door. I picked up Katie and returned her to her cage for the short trip back home.

We had barely arrived back home and gone inside when there was a loud rumble of thunder and a few seconds later a flash of lightning. I looked at my watch. It was already late afternoon and was almost time to start my evening meal. I fed the cats first, and then as a small treat, I gave each of them a small amount of whipped cream.

"Gimme, gimme!" Reilly said, whipped cream around his mouth giving him a comical look.

"Sorry cats, just that much for now, in case it reacts with the medication you had today."

"Huh," Reilly growled, but accepted what I had said with surprisingly little argument. He leaped up onto the sofa and began kneading the crocheted rug. Katie leaped up beside him and started to wash him. His eyes closed in pleasure and I tiptoed away in amusement.

"Don't think I didn't know you were watching!" he called as I entered my bedroom to brush my hair.

"It's so nice to see you happy Rellly, and you too, Katie."

She chattered for a few seconds and settled down to sleep and so did Reilly. I took a peep at them and marveled yet again at their lovely colouring.

All in all it had been a most successful day, topped off with the cosy sound of rain pattering heavily on the cottage roof.

***

# CHAPTER NINETEEN

## *Songs For The Swiss*

The phone call came late one crisp and sunny morning. It was Thomas, my Swiss friend calling me from a village named Worb, about half an hour's train journey from Bern. I had spoken to him and his fiancee Ursula from time to time and it was always a thrill to receive a call from so far away. I had visited with them in the early 1990s while in Switzerland with my friend Lou. She and I had accompanied her sister Nyanne and her small baby back there so Nyanne could rejoin her Swiss husband Marcus, who had returned a few months before to seek out a new house for them.

The connection with Thomas came with the fact that Ursula happens to be Marcus' elder sister. Thomas and Ursula invited us to dinner but Lou declined, wanting to be with her sister in Munzingerstrasse, as she knew she wouldn't see her again for several years. Thomas and Ursula came to pick me up and off we went back to their modern apartment in Worb. Dinner was simple and delicious; a meat and pasta dish with side salad, and accompanied by white wine. We had shared it with Phillippe, a radio broadcaster who played the zither well, and Werner, one of those rare people who seems a misfit, but who has an encyclopedic knowledge. In his case it was on music bands. You could ask him almost anything about any band whatsoever, and he knew who the members were, who had left and who had replaced them, and what their songs were, and when they were released.

Thomas had his own band which played a mixture of blues, country, jazz and rhythm and blues. His brother Daniel did backing vocals and played saxophone and accordian brilliantly. He is a joy to listen to as is Thomas, with his lead vocals, blues harp and guitar. The three other band members are also expert musicians and all have great stage presence.

We had sat around the table and sang old songs: to my surprise many of them were songs we'd sung as children - Clementine, Valerie, and others, which I'd long forgotten about.

When the evening was over I gave Thomas and Ursula a book of my poetry as a thank you gift for the lovely evening. Thomas surprised me by saying that: "one day we might put some of your poems to music, and maybe we will change our name to Amber - after you."

I was pleased at his words but thought philosophically: if it happens it happens; if it doesn't, never mind. In the meantime, I enjoyed the added company of their two cats, a magnificent big tabby and a black cat. Unfortunately they didn't understand English, and viewed me with some suspicion until well into the evening.

**

Thomas would phone me from time to time and say they were still thinking about changing their name and were working on putting my poems to music. *That's really nice,* I'd think, but didn't dwell on it.

Until that morning in New Zealand's spring, when Thomas rang to tell me excitedly that they had put several of my poems to music and would I like to hear two of them over the phone? I was thrilled and said yes. *All the way back from Switzerland,* I thought, to the little ol' West Coast of New Zealand's South Island came my poems, put to wonderful music.

Then came the next bit. Thomas had officially changed their band name to "Amber" and they had won a major Swiss music award, which apart from the cash, won them air time in a recording studio. So they were working hard on their first CD - to be called "Breakthrough", which was to be launched the following April, in the Swiss springtime. Thomas said they would like me to be there at the launch, and would I like that? Would I, *what!* But I knew the cost would be well out of my pocket and as Thomas said they would like me to be there during their appearances at several spring music festivals I would need to be there for at least a month. I told him finances were very tight so he suggested I write some lyrics especially for them and they would pay me for them.

"I was going to ask you anyway, to do the lyrics," he said.

The lyrics I wrote for six new songs paid for my return trip to Switzerland and, with help from my friend Wendy, there would be extra money to help with day to day expenses. Thomas had asked if I would be able to stay for two months and I agreed, although I did have some reservations about being away from my cats for so long.

"What do you think of that, Reilly?" I asked excitedly.

"Humph. *Anyone* could write lyrics."

"Go ahead then, my fine furry feline. See if you can! You're far too late to write 'What's New Pussycat?' for a start!"

"Nah, I can't be bothered writing them. They'd probably say it sounded like cat-erwauling anyway!"

Katie entered the room, yawning and blinking owlishly, her big green eyes still sleepy.

"What's all the excitement about?"

"Didn't you hear? Our mother is going to *Switzerland* and will be *abandoning* us!"

"*Mother?* Reilly, you called me *mother!* How sweet! You've never done that before."

"A mere slip of the tongue. Don't get carried away with it. Are you going to leave us or can we come too?"

"No, Reilly and Katie, you can't come with me - it's over the other side of the world and you'd have to go into quarantine anyway."

"Who says so?"

"The law does, that's who!"

"Da law is a fool."

"Sometimes it is," I agreed. "But quarantine laws have to be very strict - it they weren't we could have all sorts of diseases in this country - we could even have *snakes!*"

"Snakes? Let me at 'em! I'd soon show dem who's boss!"

"Anyway cats, I've still got to think about all this. There's an awful lot to do."

"Awful lot" was an understatement. It was already fast coming to the stage when soon there wouldn't be enough work left in the area for me to cover. I had to go further and further afield to gather stories and it was becoming very uneconomic for me to do so. However, I worked very hard to do a backlog of rural stories which would have a good "shelf-life" while I was away, and I also fully intended to do rural interviews while I was in Europe.

My friend Keith offered to take both cats for me.

"What about Ginger?" I asked. "Won't his nose be put out of joint?"

Ginger was Keith's dear old cat; no prizes for guessing what colour he was!

"He'll be okay," Keith said easily.

Which is not what he'd said the previous year when I'd asked if he would like Reilly to come for a little holiday at his house. He'd been emphatic in *not* having Reilly!

"I'm not sure Keith," I said hesitantly. "My cats might run away. Remember what you said last year?"

But Keith kept insisting, ignoring what I had just said and pointing out how much it would cost me to have my cats boarding in the cattery for weeks on end, and how bored they would be. I relented, but insisted on paying him for the cat food.

I had other serious decisions to make too. Should I keep the cottage for the two months I would be away? It would be very expensive and then there was the upkeep of the lawns and my contract with the landlord said no sub-letting, so that was out. In addition, story opportunities had diminished and some of the publications I wrote for I suspected were in financial trouble due to a lack of advertising coming in to support them. Which meant it took longer for me to get paid.

When I told my friend Shelley about my trip to Switzerland she sat down hurriedly.

"You might not come back!" she said, excited for me but sad at my leaving.

"Oh yes I will. I've got my friends here and my pussycats."

I came to the conclusion however, that I would need to shift away from the Coast and head to Christchurch, over on the east coast. My friend Wendy had moved to Christchurch a few months earlier in mid-December and it looked like I had no alternative but to follow. It was a tall order to not only move from one side of the island to the other, but inform the six editors I was dealing with at the time - and their twelve publications; write a backlog of stories with a reasonable "shelf-life", pack up my gear, sell some of it off and take my cats around to Keith's place a few days before leaving, to help them settle in.

I remember coming back home wondering if I was doing the right thing, and I'd felt sad at handing official notice in to my landlord some weeks before.

The die was cast; my cats delivered to Keith; and Reilly and Ginger promptly had an argument and Reilly removed himself in a huff. I worried he might not come back.

"He'll be okay," Keith said confidently, the same as before. I wasn't so sure. Katie seemed reasonably okay but I figured that was because she is a female and would be acceptable since there was little or no rivalry. Added to that is the fact that she is not a cat with a dominant nature; indeed, quite the reverse.

The cottage was so quiet without them but I didn't have time to dwell on it for too long. Shelley and Kevin, who'd badly needed new furniture, bought my lovely oval dining table with swivel chairs, plus my velvet lounge suite and my automatic washing machine. They picked up and paid for them on the Thursday. The next morning Shelley, Kevin and their son Simon came to pick up the rest of my gear and put it on a big trailer. My precious word processor and other writing materials were carefully stowed into my sports car.

Off we all went, in convoy on the four hour trip across the island to Christchurch, where I would be staying with friend Wendy. We managed to fit my things in here and there and soon after, the energetic Shelley and Kevin were off again. I envied their amazing stamina and wished I had more of my own. However, I reminded myself that I was wont to push myself to limits and had achieved things that others only sat and thought about, so I should not be so hard on myself when my energy levels were low.

How I missed Reilly and Katie! I'd been back to Keith's house twice before leaving to see if Reilly had returned, and had also gone looking for him and had rung the local SPCA. No one had seen a cat answering Reilly's description. I'd felt like canceling my trip altogether, but Keith insisted I stop worrying - that Reilly was in a huff and would come back when he was good and ready.

"He might have gone back home!" I'd said, despairing.

"Don't worry, I'll keep an eye out for him and will check on your place after you've left, to see if he's gone back there."

I'd begged Keith to telephone the SPCA regularly, to advertise for him and to go looking for him as well. I felt I had betrayed my cat.

"*Look,*" Keith said sternly. "I told you he's in a huff because you're going without him. He'll be back in due course, you'll see."

I still wasn't so sure about that. Fortunately Katie seemed to be settling in okay, although she and Ginger didn't get on very well. I couldn't blame Ginger for venting his feelings about the whole matter, and I was also mindful of another friend's dire warning: "you'll lose them both if they go there."

But there wasn't much I could do about it now, and the new stage of my life was now set. From West to East, I was now about to embark on a new adventure.

\*\*\*

# CHAPTER TWENTY

## *Switzerland In The Spring*

After a couple of days of rest and enjoying time with Wendy, I was feeling much better. A call back to Keith to ask if Reilly had returned proved negative. Not all negative I should add, because Katie was still there and was happy enough.

"She just likes to be cuddled a lot," Keith said in his gravelly voice.

"Smart cat!" I said happily, although in the back of my mind was the thought: where's Reilly? Is he okay? Is he hungry? Then I thought of his sheer toughness, his hunting skills and his determination to survive against all odds when he was just a kitten. I hoped all those aspects of his nature would see him through, but that he wouldn't let his stubbornness stop him from returning to Keith's house. After all, I consoled myself, it wasn't as if he didn't know Keith. Indeed, Keith had borne many scratches from Reilly, had enjoyed the experience of watching Reilly with his very own birthday cake and had often remarked on how much he admired his ruggedness and great character.

Less than five days after leaving the West Coast, I was driving my car named Ruby to the airport, to leave her in a special lock-up building for cars when their owners were going to be away for extended periods. It was roughly mid-April, and cold. I had a long way to go before I would become acclimatized to Christchurch and its extremes of temperature. It wasn't like the West Coast which produced heavy rain seemingly at the drop of a hat, but at least summers and winters were averaged out; summers were not as unbearably hot, and winters were a lot milder.

Soon I was winging my way to Auckland via Japan Airlines, and from there, onto Narita International Airport near Tokyo where I stayed overnight in the airport hotel - a massive place - before heading out again late the next morning. Tokyo was hot and muggy and I developed a bad migraine which was appeased only a little after a sweet small cup of coffee at an astronomical price.

Back on board the plane, I asked for pain relievers and they, coupled with an orange drink and food soon had me feeling better. It was just prior to boarding the plane that I found out we would be stopping off at Amsterdam where we would have new tickets allocated as we would be going on a different airline - Royal Dutch Airlines. I didn't mind at all; I'd never been to Amsterdam before and I looked forward to the experience. The stopover wasn't for long, but I had enough time for a leisurely look around the airport shops. The plane flew low over the country and I had a wonderful view of the green patchwork of fields, dykes, windmills and picturesque villages. I sat with a Peruvian girl and a man from Albania, both of whom spoke excellent English. So it was a pleasant flight from Amsterdam to Zurich, where I was to be met by Thomas and Ursula.

How lovely it was to see them again, and how much catching up there was to do! But for the next few days I slept on and off, recovering from jet lag. I looked at their cats, now bigger than ever and a few years older, and I thought of my own cats and had such a rush of longing for them that I wondered how I would cope without them for the next couple of months.

But cope I did, and very well despite the constant knot of anxiety for them. There was so much to see and do, including the taking of many photographs for use with stories I intended to write. Thomas and Ursula were at work during the day and so after I had done some household chores I would go for a walk into Worb, taking my camera. Even around the apartment there were great sights to see: the dandelions, so big and golden in the lush green grass they were too good not to photograph. And the cattle, a Simmental-cross, complete with cowbells were so pretty in the spring countryside.

The launch of the CD "Breakthrough" went very well and meeting the other band members for the first time was great as they were so kind and friendly, and seemed as interested in meeting me as I was in meeting them.

We also attended a massive American European Tour concert, which featured big names such as Emmylou Harris and Trisha Yearwood.

Just prior to the concert, which was held in Zurich, I met interesting people, including a music writer who, when he shook my hand said: "oh, you are very famous here!"

"That's good to know," I said with a smile. "But it would be nice to have the money to go with it!"

The music writer smiled in return and commented simply: "that often is the way."

**

In between spending time with Ursula and Thomas and other band members, I spent time with Ursula's parents Carmen and Fritz Graf, who took me on train rides around the country - including a big ride "around the block" down to Italy, across a northern spur, stopping halfway for a look around in Domodossola, then across to Switzerland and up to Lucerne for a stop and a look around. We walked across an old bridge with a close view of a tower bridge in its medieval splendour, if you could call it that, given that the tower was for holding prisoners in during those harsh times. We would go back to Spiez, or sometimes Zurich, depending on whether Carmen and Fritz felt like going the extra distance. But that particular day we went the shorter distance back to Spiez and caught the bus back to the alpine village of Krattigen, where Carmen and Fritz lived in a relative youngster of a picturesque house, at just 200 years old. Krattigen is a picturesque village 750 metres above sea level with glorious views over Lake Thun (pronounced Toon).

**

Carmen is something of an expert on train spotting and as she and I waited one day at the station in Spiez (about 20 minutes' train ride from Bern), she would point out which trains had come from where.

We climbed aboard a train which had just arrived back from an overnight journey across part of Europe. It was warm and cosy inside.

"This is a very nice train," Carmen informed me as she made herself comfortable. "This one is from Berlin."

"I wonder if it was a German, Italian, Dutch or Swiss who kept this seat warm for me?" I remarked.

*Who's been sitting in* my *seat?* I thought.

"Maybe it was a Frenchman," Carmen replied with her serene smile, aware of many New Zealanders' distrust for the French, following the bombing some years before by French agents of the Greenpeace ship Rainbow Warrior and the consequent death of a photographer still on board at the time.

Carmen and Fritz were wonderful to travel with: patient, caring and considerate - nothing was too much trouble for them. On one particular day, several days after I'd mentioned visiting a boutique in Frutigen (where a huge annual three-day music festival is held and which we attended and in which the "Amber" band took part), Carmen and I went to the boutique. It was supposed to be spring but the day was very bleak and cold, with snow threatening. The owner of the boutique had told me at the festival that she had all sizes of clothing in store and there were sure to be garments to fit us.

However, the lady is diminutive and most of her clothing was for smaller sizes. Neither Carmen nor I can honestly be termed diminutive - not by any stretch of the imagination, and after a while I began feeling downcast. We had gone all that way to Frutigen; first by bus then by train and had a brisk walk in the cold and we had no intention of going home empty-handed.

"It is because you are so very *large* - that is why I am unable to find things to fit you," the tiny lady said, making a sweeping gesture with her hands.

After a few more comments like that, Carmen and I felt ourselves expanding by the minute. I'd found a couple of things that suited, and something for Carmen, but we were only too pleased to leave the shop.

Back at Spiez we boarded the bus to take us to the Graf home in Krattigen.

"Which seat shall we have?" I said to Carmen.

"I do not think there is a seat big enough for us very big ladies," Carmen said humorously.

I giggled and earned myself several disapproving looks from other passengers. Is it bad to be happy? I wondered, and commented on it.

"The Swiss people are very suspicious," Carmen said.

"*All* of them?"

"Not all, but many are. They are suspicious of people who look happy."

That of course, only aroused the mischief in me. A man in traditional countryside garb stared down at me through a glass partition. I looked back at him, surprised at his unsmiling scrutiny, and after we'd locked glances for several seconds I treated him to a broad smile. Not a glimmer of a smile in return; not even a flicker of his eyelashes. I fought against the urge to laugh and afterwards I asked Carmen if she had seen the man.

"Oh yes, I saw him staring at you. There are many like him. They like ladies to dress very conservatively."

Well, that is not *me*. I like a bit of colour and verve and if some of the Swiss did not approve, that was their problem. There were other things to think about - the fabulous scenery, for instance.

We dined out on the patio, looking down the valley into a scene so lovely with the ancient black trees against a lush grass and daffodils background it almost hurt the eyes. I photographed that scene, walked a few metres and snapped off another few shots, some of Lake Thun. The mountains and villages behind it were mirrored within; tiny boats appeared like toys from this height.

It was like a picture from a children's fairy tale, and so was our visit to the *schloss* (castle) and its accompanying chapel in Spiez. The castle is surrounded by magnificent gardens and ancient trees. Since the castle was built in the late fourteenth century, it is reasonable to expect that at least some of those gnarled old trees en route to the chapel are several hundred years old.

The chapel itself is over eleven hundred years old, having been built, Carmen explained, several hundred years before the castle was. Fritz, Carmen and I attended a clarinet concert within the chapel's stone walls on a bitter Sunday afternoon. The chapel sanctuary is well lit with cleverly concealed windows. On the ceiling and part way down the walls are ancient paintings, now deteriorating with the passage of time, but still beautiful nevertheless. The biblical scenes are peaceful and gentle and I'm sure I was not alone in feeling God's presence in that wonderful old building.

Natural acoustics enhanced the already-brilliant clarinet performance and we forgot about the cold after a while.

It was only when we walked back to the bus stop after the concert that we were aware of how bitterly cold the air was. On the day before, it had snowed in Bern when we were at an official opening of a new Rudolf Steiner School.

I remember the walk up the hill following a slow bus trip through an ethereal Swiss snow scene. That walk was a new experience for me; cold though it was, the muffled sound of snow falling on my umbrella was a delight. And for the first time since arriving in Switzerland, I had cold feet. Being constantly at high altitudes had meant hot, swollen feet. People had stared at me on cold days when they saw me in sandals and light clothing. Some folk near the *bahnhof* (train station) pointed; others shook their heads and shivered, obviously wondering how I could possibly walk around like that.

Maybe we Kiwis are a hardy lot I thought, or is our country simply colder overall and I had yet to become used to the Swiss climate?

\*\*

I was invited to afternoon tea by Claudia, the wife of one of the band members (Jean-Pierre) and the girlfriend of the very talented Amber saxophonist, accordionist and backing vocalist, Daniel. Another of Claudia's friends was there too; both of whom were in radio. I was asked to sign up as a radio journalist but was told I would have to be very sure that it was what I wanted to do as although the money was excellent, the hours were long and the minimum contract I could sign up for was five years. Too long I thought, and I declined, although I was flattered to have been asked.

I was in the village of Worb one beautiful spring Saturday after the snow had temporarily cleared. I traveled in a group, traveling by horse and dray to a restaurant in a tiny village on the outskirts of Bern.

The group consisted of most of the members of the Canadian country music band Prairie Oyster; members of the Amber band and their wives and partners, the wife of the man who runs Der Braurerie (The Brewery, where Zwickel Beer and honey beer is made) and who acted as tour guide, the driver and myself.

The scenery was so perfect it was like being within a living picture postcard; I was mindful of the old and the new - the driver cheerful, strong and ruddy-cheeked with generations of farmers in his ancestry, and late model cars banking up behind us while waiting for the right opportunity to pass.

With gentle green slopes and colourful wildflowers growing in profusion as a backdrop, the Volvos, Saabs and Peugeots seemed an intrusion. When they all had passed us, the only sounds were birds in the background, the clip-clop of the horses' hooves and the jangling of the harnesses. We clip-clopped through wooded areas with daffodil-clad embankments and lush green grass carpeting the area between trees which appeared to have been planted there at the dawning of time. It was almost too much beauty to absorb at once.

Several of the band members told me that they were blown away by the ancient history of Switzerland; the castles, architecture and culture in general. Like us, their European history is still a relative baby.

They were "blown away" too, when they saw how the Swiss make the most of country music festivals. Out come the Stetsons, the fringed jackets and jeans, high-heeled boots, spurs and holsters...and in some cases, even guns. That concerned me and I asked one of the organizers of the festival about it. "Do not worry," he said. "Most of the guns are only replicas." I noticed he'd said "most", and I still felt uneasy. There is no way guns, replica or not, would have been allowed at a music festival in New Zealand, I thought. But then, this was Switzerland and things were done differently here and I had to accept that fact.

It was strange seeing the Swiss dress up like cowboys and cowgirls - certainly not the image we Kiwis have - that of the all-American or Australian cowboy.

I wondered what Reilly would make of it all.

"Damn silly if you ask me!"...I could almost hear him saying. My heart gave a lurch at the thought of my cats. I made an effort to put my feelings aside.

Finally, we stopped at a centuries-old farmhouse where we were met by another farmer - again strong and sturdy with a wide smile - and a glass of Schnapps.

"You haf der Schnapps?" he asked me and when I said "nein, danke," his big face fell. He looked so woebegone I relented and agreed, measuring with my fingers as to the very small amount I wanted in the tiny glass. I soon realized why the drink is served in tiny glasses and is called Schnapps. My head snapped back in shock, and with my throat on fire I smiled bravely and said: "ist gut", adding to myself: for a bad dose of 'flu, that is! The farmer beamed with pleasure at my words and I quietly breathed fire for the next few minutes, and hoped my heart would stop its racing. It did, but it took a few minutes.

We may have an image of the Swiss as wearing traditional dress and yodeling, and while this is so on special occasions, the Swiss, like most people in the world, have a great interest in sport. When it comes to football, their enthusiasm is second to none. On the day I was to leave Switzerland, my friend Ursula took me in their van to the bahnhof, where I was to catch the train to the Zurich airport.

The bahnhof was packed with spectators, football teams and fans. Some of the teams came in slowly, beating drums in rhythm; some simply shouted, others talked loudly and clapped. But noisiest of all and the most attention-getting was the team in colourful national costume which walked very slowly, swinging huge cowbells from side to side in unison. The din was unbelievable.

"Such fools," said Ursula, who is a trained nurse and radiographer and sees many sporting injuries in the course of her work. "There will be permanent damage to their ears."

"And ours too, "I replied, grimacing.

"They are very silly with this football. It is too dangerous."

Danger aside, the Swiss were intent on making the most of the excitement and drama of the football games, scheduled to be played that afternoon.

"We will probably see some of these people in the hospital tomorrow," Ursula said wearily. "Some will have very bad injuries."

I said that I hoped not, but knew she was probably right.

**

Soon I was winging my way back to New Zealand, my first stop: Amsterdam. While waiting for our next boarding call, I thought of the vast distances between countries and yet how small the world can be with all its God-incidences. A Dutchman who came to sit at our table in the 643-year-old-plus Lion Hotel in Worb was a salesman for farm equipment. He was both amused and astounded to hear that I wrote for a number of rural newspapers and magazines (one which specialized in farming equipment) on the other side of the world. And when I named the magazine specializing in farm equipment news and advertising he told me that their company had regular dealings with that magazine.

I thought too, of the New Zealander I'd met. A bright, bubbly red-haired woman, she teaches English to adult Swiss people - including Fritz and Carmen, and happily chats in Swiss-German as easily as in English. Helen is married to a Swiss man she met while on a tramping weekend in New Zealand.

To my pleasure, Helen told me she had taught for a year in Cobden, just over an hour's drive from where I had been living on the West Coast of New Zealand's South Island.

For want of a better phrase, I said it sure is a small world.

Helen agreed.

***

# CHAPTER TWENTY ONE

## *New Zealand A Foreign Country*

Much as I enjoyed my time in Switzerland and was sorry to say goodbye to my Swiss friends, I was anxious to return to New Zealand and pick up my cats. I had written to Keith several times while I was away, asking about them. Although Katie was fine, he said in a return letter, Reilly had not returned. Keith had gone looking for him and had phoned the SPCA several times. Somehow I couldn't believe that was the last I would see of Reilly. He seemed too vital, too full of mischief and chauvinistic behaviour, not to suddenly appear and say something like: "What are you staring at! Anyone would think you hadn't seen me for a while!"

On my return to New Zealand, I thought over the problems that could arise with having two cats to stay at my friend Wendy's townhouse, which is situated on an extremely busy street in one of Christchurch's outer suburbs. I thought Reilly might be unhappy there and I vowed to find a place of my own as soon as it was practical to do so.

There was a bitter wind moaning and sighing forlornly around the Christchurch airport when I returned in June. It felt as if I had been away for so long that New Zealand was no longer my home country. I rang the free number for my car to be brought to me and soon after it was. It was good to see Ruby again and load my things back into her, and escape the sudden drop of the back hatch before it hit me on the head. I'd never got around to having the hydraulics repaired.

Wendy gave me a friendly welcome home and handed my mail to me. After two months away there was a huge stack that had to be attended to and this I did. It was a real winding down time and presently I made an escape to bed, taking a hot water bottle with me. Later on in the afternoon I phoned my friends, including Keith back in Westport - to let them know I was back home in New Zealand. Keith told me Katie was fine but Reilly still had not returned. My heart sank. A few days later I was off back to the West Coast to catch up with friends and to seek out Reilly for myself.

Katie looked well, but I was upset to hear that she too, had run away and had been found down North Beach, tangled in a flea collar Keith had put on her. Still, for all that, she looked well and happy enough, but acted as if she didn't know me. I was ecstatic to see her and told her so. I could feel her warming towards me again.

"Why were you away so long?"

"I had so much to do! And I went an awful long way. I've been to five different countries!"

"I don't care about that. I just wanted you back home, Mum. I really missed you and I really missed Reilly too."

"Where do you think he might be?" I asked sadly.

"You're not *talking* to her, are you?" said Keith, amused.

"Of course I am! She understands me very well."

Keith gave me a bemused look, one I had often seen in the past.

I placed an advertisement, accompanied by a picture of Reilly, in the local newspaper. There were several replies. I answered them, but no, not one was Reilly, or even remotely like him despite the clear photo I had submitted with the advertisement. Each time the phone rang at my friend's place I dared to hope it might be someone with some good news of my much-loved cat. Hope dies hard - as the saying goes. Part of me tried to resign to the fact that I might never see Reilly again, but there were other times when the image of him was so strong, I could not give up on my search. I rang the SPCA office staff so many times their voices had a resigned note in them as soon as they recognized my voice.

I tried not to be discouraged, but a blanket of depression began to settle over my shoulders. I missed Reilly dreadfully - I even missed his sarcastic remarks. He'd turned my life upside down when he entered it and now my life was turned upside down again because he was missing. A thousand times I berated myself for not putting both cats in the cattery. So what if it had cost me several hundred dollars for their board and lodgings while I was away and they had been extremely bored? At least I would still have them both!

My friend Eileen, who had been my neighbour the previous year, phoned to say she'd seen the ad in the paper.

My heart soared.

"Have you seen Reilly?"

"I thought I did. P'raps you'd better come out here and we'll go for a walk down the beach. We might find him on the way."

With my heart swelling with hope, I drove out to Carter's Beach, wishing I'd never left the place, and visited Eileen. It was great to see her and her husband George again. Eileen possesses a rare brand of humour and I found her a very stimulating person to be with. While George carried on sawing up wood, Eileen and I went for a walk down the beach. It was a cold day but the beach on a cold day had never worried Reilly before and it wasn't likely to now. With a lot of hope, timing and good luck, maybe he'd be there today, hiding in the pampas at the beach front, just waiting to leap out at us and say *"boo!"*

It felt very strange being back at the beach; I still had that slight feeling of being displaced - as if I was in a foreign country. Fortunately the feeling was leaving me gradually, but coming from a glorious European spring into a bleak New Zealand winter and knowing a beloved cat is missing, does not a cheerful woman make.

Eileen and I looked in all sorts of places and called for Reilly over and over. Not a trace of him could be found and as the afternoon wore on my heart became very heavy. We headed back to Eileen's house where I thanked her for her time and company, and drove back to my friend's home.

A sunny day dawned the next day, and with it my spirits had lifted again. It was time to have another look in the near vicinity.

Out I went for a walk down the street...and there coming towards me was a cat who looked so much like Reilly...*surely not?* I dared to hope again and then I heard that distinctive voice as the cat ran along in the kerbing.

"I have fought on the beaches - Carter's Beach to be exact, and I have fought in the trenches!"

"*Reilly!*" I squealed in sheer joy and ran towards him and swept him up in my arms, tears pouring down my face. "Oh my baby, my darling cat! Where have you *been?*"

"Stop fussing, woman! I've been...oh, everywhere! Just like *you!*" And he glared at me. "How *dare* you go away and leave us like that!"

"I had to take the chance!" I said defensively. "Shout at me, rage at me Reilly - I don't care! I'm just so pleased to have you back with me!"

He twisted around in my arms and I couldn't help but notice he was grubby and a lot thinner. His great golden eyes focused on my face.

"Maybe I don't *want* to come home with you anymore. Maybe I just like running wild!"

I smooched up against him. "Oh my dear pussycat. Didn't you miss me? And Katie?"

"Maybe I did, and maybe I didn't."

"I smooched into his fur, dirty as it was. "Oh go on Reilly - didn't you miss us just an eensy teensy bit?"

"Well...yes, I have to admit to a certain fondness for you both but I sure didn't like that place you took me to!"

"But you know Keith and you had Katie with you!"

"Yeah, but I didn't like dat ginger thing he had there - dat thing dat poses as a cat!"

"Remember you were on his territory."

175

"Ghastly, inhospitable cat! Anyway, it was time I went walkabout. There was so much to see and do."

"Do you want to get down again?"

He sank into my shoulder and began purring.

"Actually, I quite like it here. Maybe I *will* come back with you. You owe me a dance, woman, and I need a Katie O'Brien fix."

"What do you mean by that?" I stroked his fur and felt the grime on my hands.

"I haven't picked on her for a while. Yes, there are things I need to catch up on."

"You'll have to come to Christchurch with me."

"First things first, woman. Just be glad I've come back to you. It's a big, exciting world out there and I'm a strong advocate of the call of the wild."

"Whatever you say my darling. Come to Keith's with me and see if we can get a few things sorted out with Ginger."

"I hate him. I hate dat cat. He reminds me of that fat cat Misty who lived next door."

"Yes well, they're the same colour. Ginger possibly hates you too, but if you let him know you'll only stay for a little while, perhaps he'll mellow a bit."

"Pigs might fly, but I'll give it a try - hey! I'm a poet again! Put me up a tree again woman, and I'll be a poet-tree cat! Oh, aren't I a character!"

"You're a wonderful, marvelous, adorable cat and I love you very much."

"Yeah, dat's me, Reilly - a dreadful, adorable cat!"

"I've heard that a few times too!" I said happily, and began walking to Keith's house.

Ginger was waiting to greet us.

"Hiss, dirty grey cat."

"Hiss yourself, O Ginger One. My person says I've got to explain to you that I'm not stopping for long."

"Just as well. This is *my* territory."

"You is an inhospitable ginger thingy of a cat."

"Hiss. I am known as a red tabby, and a fine specimen I am too, even if I do say so myself!"

"Stick yer under my human's mop of hair and you'd never find you! You match her hair."

"I should go home with your human, then."

"Naw, she's *mine!* I've only just found her again. You keep yer ginger paws off her!"

"Hiss. Who do you think you are, coming to my house and ordering me around?"

"Seamus O'Reilly, dat's who! I hope you haven't been picking on my girlfriend while I've been away!"

Ginger sat on his haunches and began washing his face. Then he yawned. I had seen Reilly apply the same tactics of assumed boredom.

"Actually, since she's living with me, I rather think that makes her *my* girlfriend, don't you?"

"Hiss! She's *mine!*"

"Hiss, spit!"

Just then, Katie appeared in the doorway and gave an appealing little meow.

"Boys, boys, are you fighting over me? Reilly, how wonderful to see you again! How I have missed you! Why did you run away? I was heartbroken!"

"Questions, questions! Why do females want to know so much?"

"Because they're females," Ginger said, his gaze swiveling from Katie to Reilly and back again. "You're not going to two-time me, are you Katie O'Brien?"

"But I was never your girlfriend, Ginger. Besides, you told me you didn't like me much."

"That was just to keep you in your place. I really think you're marvelous."

"You never said so! We girls like to be told how you feel about us - *truly* feel about us, that is!"

"Can't have you taking us for granted," Ginger replied.

Reilly yawned when I put him to the ground. He really did look exhausted.

"Look guys, I need to stay a night or two before our human takes us to Christchurch. But I won't bore you with the details."

Ginger looked at him warily. "Providing it's understood that this is *my* territory."

"Yes, O Ginger One, dis is *your* territory - I agree to dat in front of witnesses!"

Ginger was mollified and let a smirking Reilly in the front door where Keith was standing, grinning at the look on my face.

"Told you he'd be back when he was good and ready!"

I looked up at him. "Yes Keith, you did."

"And what a worry wart you were too!"

Reilly looked at me smugly from the doorway. I knew it pleased him to hear I was really worried about him.

"An' I'm on Ginger's territory an' all!"

He moved away to explore the other rooms. I am sure I heard him call out "suckers!" before he went down the hallway.

Really, nothing much had changed at all.

***

# CHAPTER TWENTY TWO

## *Life In The Big City*

By no means did our trip to Christchurch go smoothly. It was a bitter day and I was concerned about the possibility of snow in the Lewis Pass. There was. I hated driving through snow - much as I admire its stark whiteness and beauty as it hangs in the trees and sparkles in the sunlight, I would prefer to be walking in it - preferably with well-shod feet, and enjoy the delicious crunching underfoot. Alas, the novelty of snow wears off very quickly! Several times I felt my car fishtail and my cats squeaked with fright.

"Dis is not a race track, woman!"

"I know, I know. I'm doing the best I can, and I am going slow." But even at slow speeds, negotiating the Lewis Pass in winter is a hazardous experience. "However, I do recall you asking me if this was supposed to be a sports car..."

"Different circumstances, different time."

I glanced at him in the rear vision mirror. As expected, he had a lofty look on his face. That cat has the gall of Old Nick, I'd swear to it...that's if swearing was one of my fortés, which it isn't.

Finally we were through and on the last leg of the four hour trip which had been extended by half an hour due to the weather conditions. I was bone weary by the time we arrived, and as Wendy had to go out that night, it was just me, Reilly and Katie at the house. Katie was still groggy from the tranquilizer but Reilly was full of curiosity about his surroundings. I was afraid he might knock over Wendy's pretty figurines but by carefully removing them to safer places and generally keeping a watchful eye on my curious cat, I managed to avert disaster.

It was kind of Wendy to put us up but I knew it would be just short weeks away before I'd have to leave and take my still-packed belongings with me. It was very tricky trying to write stories with boxes packed around me and having to kneel on the floor in a confined space to update my scrapbook - a very necessary part of my work.

"Say one for me while you're down there," Reilly often said.

"I may never rise again," I would reply.

"Dat is a very cheeky thing to say to a fine upstanding cat!"

"So sit down, cat," I would respond to that remark, and often as not Reilly would go off in a huff.

I had answered an advertisement for a flat in The Press, a Christchurch-based newspaper that covered the South Island, and one which I'd worked for while based in Westport. I called the lady who'd advertised, just before leaving the West Coast with my cats on that cold day, and although the flat was not immediately available, the lady was interested in me, and later told me the flat was mine to rent.

Moving day came, with help from friend Jeff, who was in a tetchy mood.

"Hurry up; I haven't got all day!" he snapped.

"Neither have I!" I retorted, mindful that I had offered to help him shift, and which I did, twice. And both times those house moves were fraught with problems.

"Uh-oh Katie, dem two's at loggerheads again."

"It does not bode well, Reilly."

I did as much of the work as possible and thanked Jeff by buying some delicious take-away food and reiterating my promise to help him shift again - when the time came. That cheered him up and off he went.

"Phew!" I said as I sat back on the sofa to relax. I felt as much worn out by the move as by coping with Jeff's mercurial moods.

"Dat is dat," said Reilly, after he'd inspected the flat from top to bottom and Katie had done the same, and they'd plonked themselves down on the sofa with a big sigh. Anyone would have thought they'd played a major part in the shifting of the furniture.

"I heard you think dat. We *did* play a major part...we inspected all da goods."

"So you did," I smiled.

I made up a litter box for them to use, so they didn't go outside too soon, and we began our first evening together in our new flat.

**

And so began our new life in the big city - or at least in the suburbs. Just finding my way around was a big enough task and I found driving in the city traffic exhausting. It was always a joy to come home and relax with the cats. Fortunately for us all, we were only a short walk from the beach.

"But it's not the same!" said Reilly, who hated the many people who also liked to go to the beach.

"Of course it's not. We're on the East Coast now."

"Well, I don't like it here. I wanna go back to the other side. What about *you,* Katie?"

"Oh it's not so bad, Reilly..." and when Reilly rubbed up against her and started washing her, she added: "but it would be *really* nice to go back to Carter's Beach!"

*Traitor!* I thought. "Let's put it this way kitty-cats; there is little work for me over there now and as I am by no means a rich lady, I have to earn my living the best way I can - by writing for magazines and newspapers."

"Yeah, but you know you're bored by it."

"How did you know *that?"*

"I've heard you sighing sometimes when they give you a boring story to do and a short deadline!"

"You are a very smart cat, Reilly."

"Haven't I always told you that?"

181

"Yes you have." I stroked his wonderful fur and for once he didn't seem to mind me doing that. Leonardo da Vinci referred to the cat as "Nature's Masterpiece". *How right he was,* I thought. I wished sometimes that humans could have more of the cat's attributes; a keen perception, agility, elegance and individuality. It was Mark Twain who first said that if Man could be crossed with a cat it would improve Man, but it would deteriorate the cat. Mark Twain might have been the first to say it, but I am more than happy to repeat it!

Katie rubbed up against me. She wasn't saying much; she left most of the talking to Reilly but she had her tried-and-true ways of getting her message across. Often it was her habit of leaping onto the dining table, knowing I was going to immediately pick her up off it. It was one way of ensuring she got an extra cuddle out of me.

If she was in the mood to go to the beach and I wasn't in the mood, she would gaze at me with her enormous green eyes; so much was said in that gaze. She didn't need to open her mouth. I wondered and not for the first time, if she was picking up on Reilly's habits. Were they beginning to gang up on me - for the mere fact I am a member of the human species? It was possible, although cats are not usually wont to bite the hand that feeds them, so to speak. Although now that I think of it, I have known cats who were more than happy to bite the hand that fed them...maybe it was their way of saying: "how about a decent bit of variety in our food?" Jerome K. Jerome, the English writer could have been speaking to me about Katie when he made this statement: "a cat's got her own opinion of human beings. She don't say much, but you can tell enough to make you anxious not to hear the whole of it."

I shared his opinion too. I explained to Katie that the times I did not want to go to the beach were times when I felt it was prudent not to.

"Why?" she asked beseechingly, and Reilly added his own beseeching "Why?"

Cats are champions at beseeching. I would like to demote beseeching to groveling, to put it in a better perspective, but it seems that cats also have a knack of turning any situation around - no matter how bad or cunning they have been - to put themselves back on top.

"Why?" Reilly beseeched again. I stared at him; looking for signs of actual groveling. He blinked innocently: there was no groveling to be detected.

"Instinct," I replied. "Sometimes I feel it's not safe to take you."

"Not safe for *dogs,* woman!" Reilly growled.

A man came to the door and knocked.

"Burglars! Robbers! Let me at 'em!" Reilly declared and, lowering his haunches, he prepared to spring as I was about to open the door.

"They're hardly likely to come a-knocking," I said quickly.

"Could be a double-bluff!" said Reilly, and his instincts were not too far wrong. When I warily opened the door I had to look around to the side, where a very dubious-looking young man stood. His action alone of staying out of sight spoke volumes. Reilly stood at the door with me, growling, glaring and swishing his tail.

"Is Andrew here?" the young man said in almost guttural tones; the tones and body language of a man used to staying on the wrong side of the law. I replied no, that no-one of that name lived here, and off he went. Months later he returned and acted in the same way, saying the same thing as if his previous visit had never been. Maybe it hadn't, as far as he was concerned. I suspected that he was on drugs and Reilly growled at him; glared and swished his tail the way he'd done on the man's first visit. The man looked askance at Reilly, gave me a strange look and left. I said some very fervent prayers that night and was not at all surprised to find out not long afterwards that drug dealers used to live in the flat.

"Thieves, robbers and vagabonds!" Reilly stated when I told him about the previous tenants. "I knew I was right the first time!"

"Yes you were," I said tenderly. "You're better than any watchdog."

"Too right I am! Even Katie will agree to that."

Katie looked at him adoringly. "I would much rather have you than a dog," she said sweetly. Reilly lowered his head and looked at her suspiciously. Katie blinked owlishly in return and began purring and kneading at the carpet. Reilly was mollified.

The young man never returned, thankfully. Normally healthy people who throw their good health away by indulging in drugs and putting other people's lives at risk too, are not my favourite people by any means...but that's another story.

**

"Seamus O'Reilly, come here pussycat," I said one morning several days later. I was armed with a brush and comb. Reilly took one look at the weapons I had in my hand, and sat rigid in the chair.

"Brushing I can tolerate for 30 seconds, but combing I will not tolerate for *one* second!"

"But Reilly, Katie's had a brushing and now it's your turn. Besides, your ruff is matted and it spoils your good looks."

He was suspicious of my back-handed compliment.

"Listen here woman. Do you know what my initials are? Well you should do, since you named me - more or less. But in case it's slipped your mind they are ess, oh, ar. Dat spells sor...or *sore,* which is what I will be if you attack me with dat comb. When my ruff disturbs me too much, I shall thin it out by myself, thank you very much."

That was a longer-than-usual bit of dialogue for him.

"Sore rhymes with Thor," I mentioned casually - the thought just coming to me.

"I like dat! Thor is a god of thunder...or whatever...yeah, yeah, dat's *me!*"

"But you are terrified of thunder, cat," I reminded him.

"I can change my mind, can't I? Watch me soar through the air on a thunderbolt!"

With a loud growl he launched himself into the air and tried to reach the sofa on the opposite side of the small lounge room. He just missed and landed with a thud directly in front of the sofa, bumping his jaw on it.

"Thor is now sore," I said succinctly. Reilly gave me an evil look and stalked out of the room, his head held high.

"I hate puns," Reilly said as he walked rigid-legged around the corner into the next room. It was easy to detect he was now in a snit with me.

I giggled and Katie looked at me, almost sternly.

"He could have hurt himself, Mum."

"He shouldn't have been showing off then, should he?"

Katie gave me no answer to that; she just sat and gave herself a washing to show me my remark had been of no consequence whatsoever. I went into the small kitchen-dining area where Reilly was calmly cleaning up his food bowl as if my comments just a moment before been deleted from his memory banks. When he saw me he gave several chirrups and a swish of his tail, and made a beeline for the lounge. I followed him back in there and sat on the sofa in amusement, watching Reilly - now on the chair opposite, pulling out clumps of his thick ruff and spitting them onto the floor.

"Have it your way, cat," I said.

"I intend to, my good woman. Look at this mess you have to clean up!"

"You should be cleaning it up yourself, pussycat, since you're the one making the mess."

He stopped his spitting and tugging for a moment to gaze at me in astonishment - or maybe it was assumed astonishment.

"You expect a cat such as *I* to clean up after me? My good woman, please do remember that I am an answer to your prayers! You should feel *privileged* to clean up after me!"

"Sarcastic sod," I muttered darkly, and left the room.

It didn't surprise me to hear that distinctive sniggering again.

\*\*\*

# CHAPTER TWENTY THREE

## *On The Move Again*

The flat was too small for us: when visitors came there seemed little room left to move around in. When Jeff came to visit, being a big man he dwarfed the place even more. One day he visited and was in one of his snits for whatever reason, and was trying my patience.

"You have da patience of a saint," Reilly said to me out in the kitchen-dining area, where I was making cups of coffee. "Want me to bite him hard?"

"Yeah, why not?" I said, exasperated by Jeff's moods. Glancing out the kitchen window I heard boys shouting out on the road. Since Jeff's lovely new car was parked out front I thought I'd better investigate. Jeff was still muttering away and for the umpteenth time I wondered why I tolerated him...and for the umpteenth time I told myself it was because he is the brother of a friend.

I went outside and stopped to watch what the boys were up to. Reilly was by my side, his tail swishing. The boys were doing what boys have done down the centuries - throwing a ball to one another. The ball landed on the grass berm next to where Jeff's car was parked, and rolled underneath. The boy knelt down to retrieve the ball and although I couldn't hear what he said, I could lip read and the body language was wonderful. He put his hand to the ground to steady himself as he looked under the car, was suddenly aware of putting his hand in something soft and sat back to see what it was. "*Ugh...*yuk! *Dog* shit!" I lip-read. The boy frantically wiped his hand on clean parts of grass and kept sniffing at his hand to ensure he'd got the offending material off. And then to finish off, he wiped his hand down his shorts... all the better for his mummy to know what he'd got himself into. Maybe that's what the writers mean, I thought, when they say "the distinctive smell of boy".

"Dat boy is really on the ball and in the poo!" Reilly sniggered.

I giggled. "I thought you didn't like puns," I reminded him.

"Today I do."

I collected my bottles of milk from the milk box and, still chuckling, I followed Reilly inside.

"What's so amusing?" said Jeff, his tone still sulky.

"Dog poo," I said and laughed loudly.

"Harumph! Doesn't take much to amuse *you!*" he snarled. "Small things amuse small minds!"

"Yes!" I retorted. "But small minds take *notice!*"

Reilly and I went snickering into the other room, where I finished making coffee.

"Dat man is a jerk," Reilly commented. "I don't know how you put up with him."

"I really don't know why, either, apart from the fact he's the brother of a friend."

"Talking to yourself again?" Jeff snarled, his voice lightly muffled by the sound of the television which he'd just switched on, without having the courtesy to ask me if I minded.

"Why not?" I called. "I'm one of the few people *I* can have a sensible conversation with!"

"And me," Reilly added.

"Yes you too, Reilly. I agree."

"And me!" piped little Katie.

"Indeed, sweetheart," I said.

"You'd better watch out or those men in their long white coats will come and take you away!" Jeff called from the lounge room.

"Don't be surprised if it's *you* they come to take away!" I snapped, many times having been on the receiving end of Jeff's mercurial moods.

"One of these days I'm going to bite dat man," Reilly said darkly.

"Be my guest," I said. "And make it a really hard bite while you're at it!"

Reilly promptly went into the small lounge and although I didn't see him do it, the yelps and snarls told me a great deal.

"Ow! Your bloody cat bit me on my ankle!" Jeff yelled. "Get off!"

I chuckled happily. "Be thankful he didn't bite you anywhere else."

"I'm getting outa here!" Jeff yelled. "You and your cats are *mad!*"

"Dat sounds like the pot calling the kettle black," Reilly said in a muffled tone. I realized why when he entered the small kitchen/dining area and started spitting out bits of cloth.

"You're right, Reilly," I said, moving slowly to the lounge room, where Jeff was looking furious and nursing his ankle.

"You should get rid of that cat! Look at this! He's *ruined* my good trousers!" Jeff said, his face red with anger and his hair seeming to stick up on end, as it was wont to do when he was in a bad mood. "He should be reported to the authorities!"

At that, Reilly ran back into the lounge and leaped at him and raked his claws down his arm.

"How dare you speak about me like dat!"

"Yes indeed, Jeff, how dare you speak about Reilly like that? You've really upset him!"

"I wouldn't be surprised if you deliberately set him onto me!" Jeff shouted. He rubbed his arm which was oozing blood and then his ankle – it too was oozing blood - and limped over to the armchair where he'd dumped his jacket. "I'm going and won't be back!"

"Oh dear, oh dear, never mind," I said with a smile. My smile grew wider when I saw that the boys playing ball had accidentally lobbed it right into the remaining dog poo on the berm. One of the boys promptly kicked the ball out, but with a bit of the offending material stuck to the ball, it changed direction and hit Jeff's lovely black car, leaving a trail down the side of the door.

I was pleased that I had seen the action, and luckily for the boys they ran away just as Jeff was flouncing out the door and he didn't see them. Luckily too, he didn't see the mark down the passenger door, or he would have blamed that on Reilly.

Jeff drove away furiously with a squeal of his tyres and a few seconds later I heard a siren, which I assumed was a police siren. I kept watching and sure enough it was. A police car, lights flashing, roared past my flat and tooted. I hoped it was at Jeff. I slowly went out the front of my flat and did a cursory check of my mailbox while looking up the street. I could see an angry Jeff gesturing at the policeman, who was wagging his finger at him. I knew that wouldn't go down well with the bad-tempered Jeff, and oh, surprise surprise, I could hear shouting and a moment later another police car arrived.

"Dis is exciting!" Reilly said as he twirled around my ankles. "It looks like dat man has got what he deserves."

"No doubt it will all get blamed on us," I said. "Don't be surprised if the police come here looking for us."

"Naw, dat man will be too busy trying to talk his way out of a ticket for speeding. And maybe they'll add a bit more on for not co-operating wid the cops!" Reilly padded right out onto the footpath. "Yep, what did I tell you? Can you hear dat shouting? They're taking him away! He's probably shouting that it's all a cat's fault, namely mine!"

I chuckled heartily. "I knew his bad temper would get him into trouble sooner or later."

"Yeah, but da cops have the wrong clothes on."

"What do you mean?"

"They should be wearing white coats!"

His meaning was very clear.

"Yes, to take Jeff away to the funny farm."

When we went back inside, Katie came out from the bedroom, yawning.

"What's been happening while I've been sleeping?"

"You missed some excitement, Katie! Let me tell you..." and he steered her back into the bedroom to tell her all about it.

**

The incident with Jeff gave our spirits a temporary uplift, but it wasn't for long. High rents, short-term accommodation and lack of space meant I had to move thrice more before I found a place I really liked. It was a case of taking what was affordable in the meantime, even though it wasn't necessarily what I would have liked.

"Make up yer mind woman, where we'll be going next."

"I'm doing my best, cat! It's not *you* paying the rent!"

"I wanna go back to the Coast."

"We *are* on the Coast!"

"Yeah, but not the Coast I like. We hardly go to the beach and when we do it's not the same!"

"Do you think I don't know that?"

"Then why all dis fussing about, shifting us here, shifting us dere! I tell you, it's not good for us pussycats...especially *me!*"

He looked so forlorn that I had to pick him up and cuddle him. He immediately sank into my shoulder and began to purr. It had been a while since he did that; it was like old times again. I leaned over to turn on the stereo and soon the rich tones of Chris Rea filled the room.

"Dat man stirs a pussycat's soul," Reilly said.

I laughed and agreed. Katie opened one huge green eye at us and resumed her nap on the sofa, sighing in her sleep.

"See, even Katie O'Brien is dreaming about the Coast."

I realized suddenly what all Reilly's closeness was about. He was trying to worm his way around me into moving back to the West Coast.

"I've got your number, cat. If we move back to the West Coast, how would we live? Who would pay the bills?"

His claws sank into my shoulder. "*You* would, woman," he said succinctly. "You would get a job."

190

"Oh would I now? What have I been doing all these years, with never a full weekend off?"

"Writing stories on boring subjects...yeah yeah, I know all about it!"

"How do you know?" I demanded, diverted yet again.

"It's you, woman! It's not hard to tell. You're restless - and so am I! I wanna go back to da Coast!"

I put him to the floor and walked into the next room. He'd got me thinking hard about the possibility of going back to the West Coast. But the bottom line was one of the reasons for our having shifted away in the first place - lack of work opportunities and high unemployment. No, much as the peace, relaxed lifestyle and the friendliness of the Coast people attracted me, the fact remained that I still had to earn a living.

I turned to see Reilly watching me from the lounge doorway. "Besides," I added, as if I had spoken my earlier thoughts aloud, "who would feed you cats if I had no money for food?"

"We would scavenge, woman!"

"You would not! You like your home comforts far too much!"

He sniffed the air in a pompous manner and turned his back to me. "I shall not reply to that remark."

"Okay, let's compromise...I *need* a job to keep a roof over our heads and food in our tummies. How about we move to one more place in Christchurch, and that will be our last place there. If it doesn't work out - we move back across the island. There is no work over there for me right now - I'd gone as far as I could, but that's not to say there won't be another job in - maybe another six months..."

"Woman, you sure can talk a lot!" Reilly interrupted. His tone had softened, however.

"Does this mean we have a compromise?"

"If you say so. But for the record, please note I am going with you under protest."

"What about you, Katie?"

She opened her eyes and yawned.

"I'll go where you go, Mum."

"Have you no *spine*, Katie O'Brien? Hey! I'm a poet again!"

His brief uplift was that - brief. He did not want to be seen to be coming around too soon, to my way of thinking.

Katie yawned again. "Of course I have a spine, Reilly. I just don't like to go around like a roaring lion, like *you* do. I have *other* methods!"

"Well said, Katie!" I applauded, and Reilly went off in another huff, muttering "women!" Indeed, it was his chauvinism that went with him "like a roaring lion". Despite that, he was adorable, and knew it.

"I *hear* you!" he called from the other room.

"Hear all you like, cat, even my thoughts," I called back. "We move in a month. Okay?"

"I suppose it will have to be. I will remind you again to take note I have registered my protest and therefore my disapproval of da whole idea."

"Fair enough. Now we've made the decision..."

"No, *you* made the decision!" Reilly interrupted, as he so often did. "*We* just have to go along wid it!"

"'The die is cast...'" I began to quote.

"Yeah, yeah, and all dat guff," Reilly interrupted again. "I'm going out. Coming, Katie?"

Katie yawned once more, rose to her paws and stretched luxuriously, and leaped nimbly from the sofa to Reilly's side.

"Where are we going?"

"To the beach, small cat. Who knows, it may be our last trip for a long time."

"Ooo, Reilly, surely not?" She turned her great green gaze on me, and with Reilly's golden gaze on me as well, I stood there feeling accused and ganged up on.

"I have no choice," I said lamely. "In any case, you don't particularly like the beach here."

"Huh!" Reilly sniffed. In that one small exclamation he managed to portray a great deal.

In unison they turned their backs on me and walked slowly to the door for me to let them out. Without another word they left, to explore places unknown for an hour or two. I sighed, and thought about the task ahead. My cats didn't understand how tired I was of shifting. I had tried to explain that it went with my sort of territory. There was much truth in the old comments about writers and artists starving in garrets - and while we weren't exactly starving, it was a constant worry whether I would have enough money to meet the next fortnight's rent.

Not only that, my Ruby - my lovely red and deep charcoal grey Mazda RX7 was failing. Nearly six years of driving over rough back country roads had finally taken their toll. Although I'd had Ruby maintained regularly, major problems were developing, and I'd been experiencing a sense of danger for several weeks, each time I came to a busy Christchurch intersection. Ruby often stopped at these intersections and was difficult to restart. She was worse on a cold morning: scrub fires had nothing on my Ruby when it came to making smoke. I dreaded the thought that my neighbour might have hung out her washing at that hour. I visualized black smuts over pristine whiteness.

I visited numerous car sale yards and saw a few cars which appealed, but when I noted the price tag, suddenly the cars lost their appeal. I had considered having an exchange engine installed in my present car but decided that the cost of that, plus a new gearbox and having power steering installed would outweigh the cost of another car. I prayed for wisdom, pacing the floor in my small dining area. The telephone rang: it was my friend Kevin, calling from the West Coast. I told him of my dilemma and he supported my concerns. He also guessed I had already seen another car I liked, in this case a small white Japanese import, which I had taken for a drive and absolutely loved, although the price was rather high.

"If you got all that work done on your Mazda, you know what you would still have?" Kevin said.

"Yes," I sighed. "I would still have an old car, albeit with some expensive work done on it."

"Exactly. This Toyota you're talking about sounds good. Toyotas have a good reputation for reliability."

I perked up at his words.

"You're right, Kevin. I think I'll go for the little Toyota."

And so the decision was made to purchase the sports car, which was small and very fast.

With great reluctance I drove Ruby into the sale yard where I was to sign for and inspect my Japanese import before returning to pick it up the next day. I felt as if I was abandoning Ruby. That's the worst of giving a name to one's car; the car takes on real family membership.

The creaking suspension and rust in the doors convinced me, however, that I'd done the right thing, even though Reilly was furious with me.

"How *dare* you sell Ruby!" Reilly complained loudly. "Hasn't she featured in your poems? Haven't *both* Ruby and I featured in your poems?"

"Yes, pussycat, but I'm not selling *you*."

"You might as well! Oh I shall *miss* Ruby! I shall *miss* going for rides in her!"

"You can go for rides in my new car - it's a fast little sports car."

"I thought you were broke? But you can buy a new *car?*"

"It's not new. It's a few years old and I'll be paying it off and anyway I'm relying on God to supply our needs."

"Don't *work*, then! Sit on your chuff and let God supply your needs."

"Really cat, you do learn some rather uncouth expressions!"

"It's the company I keep," he said smugly. "Now, you'd better tell me about this new car. As if we didn't have enough to worry about, what with going to shift an' all!"

"First of all Reilly, let me tell you a story I'd read somewhere once about a man who wanted God to supply all his needs..." I paused, thinking about the story.

"Get on with it, woman, tell me the story - educate this poor, long-suffering cat!"

"There is no need to be sarcastic, Reilly," I replied, giving him a stern look. "There were two postmen. One went about his job and completed it for the day. He decided to check on the other postman, as he was still new to the job. He rode his bike on the route the rookie had taken but before he'd got very far, he espied the new postman sitting down on the footpath, having a rest. His mailbags were still bulging with letters.

"What do you think you are doing?" said the experienced postman.

"I'm waiting on a word from the Lord," the rookie replied.

"Oh yes? What for?"

"I'm waiting on the Lord to supply my every need."

"In that case you'd better give the Lord your entire pay packet, if you're expecting Him to do your work for you!"

He gave the rookie a stern warning about doing his job properly or else he was well and truly "on his bike" down the road and out of a job.

"So you see Reilly, God said He would supply our every need, but He gave us hands to work towards the things we need."

"Paws, in our case. Gee, you talk a lot!"

"You also need to have faith," I added.

He walked off; his parting shot was: "I'm going to say goodbye to Ruby."

He sure knew how to make me feel a heel.

**

Into the car sale yard I went, and filled out the rest of the necessary papers to take over, on hire purchase, ownership of the smart little white automatic Toyota MR2 Supercharger, complete with a targa top. I'd been for a ride in the car a few days before and was most impressed with its comfort, speed and much easier steering.

At five o'clock, during the rush hour, I took out my new car for the first time. It was with some trepidation I drove the fast little car into the busy traffic. On an eight-lane highway a few minutes later a car ran a red light while another came up fast on my left side. There was nowhere to go except very fast forward, which I did and the supercharger was all I expected it to be. If I'd still had Ruby - with her slower pick-up, I would have been hit on my side of the car for sure. My instinct of impending danger over the past few weeks had been correct. When I arrived home I thanked God for the constant little warnings and the subsequent blessing of a new car.

Reilly and Katie came out to investigate.

"Well cats, what do you think of her?"

Katie only blinked and yawned.

"It will do I suppose, even though it looks like a toy."

"You're half right, Reilly."

"What do you mean?"

"It's a Toyota!"

"Very humorous, I'm sure. Gimme a ride in it real soon, woman!"

Off he stalked, Katie following. They had accepted the new car and for that, I was thankful.

\*\*\*

# CHAPTER TWENTY FOUR

## *Vive La Difference!*

The cats had accepted the car, sniffing around it for all their worth before pronouncing it "okay".

"What will you call *dis* one?" Reilly asked.

"Maybe *carte blanche!*" I laughed.

"You are a dotty woman. Have you been called dat before?"

"What, carte blanche?"

"No, silly, a dotty woman."

"Often," I replied. "There was a time though, if I'd been seen by the neighbours, they might have phoned up the men in long white coats to come and take me away, as Jeff had suggested."

"How so?"

"It was when I was living on a hill in Nelson. We had a drought and the back lawn was cracking up. At nights you could hear the crickets – little Jiminys everywhere. They were there during the day too, making their presence known."

"Jiminy Cricket is a grasshopper."

"Yeah, I know that. Maybe in America they call crickets grasshoppers, and the other way round as well. Anyway, here were all these cute little black/brown crickets on the lawn, chirping away merrily."

"Until you came out in yer big ol' boots..."

"Don't be horrible, Reilly! I'm not like that! Anyway, I'd hardly say they were cute little things if I really thought otherwise, would I?"

"How should *I* know? There's no accounting for what a human thinks."

"Nonsense! You've often said pussycats know all, see all. Now...stop sidetracking me. I was telling you a story..."

"Well, get on with it den, woman!"

Exasperated, I glared at him and stuck my hands on my hips.

"Why is it that when you're like this, Katie is rarely around to see you?"

Reilly smirked. "Because I'm a smart cat, dat's why!"

"Anyway, as I was saying...here were all dese...er...*these* cute little black/brown crickets on the lawn, chirping away. I thought I'd like to make friends with them..."

"Why?" Reilly interrupted. He was really, really good at that.

"Just because all God's creatures are fearfully and wonderfully made."

"I'd zoom in on that word "fearfully" when applied to us cats, if I were you."

It was my turn to ask why.

"To make sure youse humans are kept in line, dat's why!"

"Charming, I must say. Anyway, here I was, out on the lawn with the crickets - well, that is, they all ducked for cover in the cracks in the lawn when I approached them, and..."

"I don't blame dem one bit!"

"Stop interrupting me, cat!"

Reilly sat back and smirked, and gave himself a quick, nonchalant wash. "You take such a long time to tell a story!"

"I wouldn't if you'd stop interrupting me all the time. So... when the crickets went to ground, so to speak, I knelt down and peered into the cracks. There they were - looking up at me, their antennae twitching madly. Fascinating little creatures, they were..."

"I wonder if dey thought dat about *you?* No, of course dey wouldn't. It would be something like: my God! A giant is invading us! A long-haired, blue-eyed creature who is as big, if not bigger dan an ant hill! To ground, chaps, to ground, I say!"

"Yessss Reilly," I said in a long-suffering tone. "Anyway, I said to them: 'ha ha! You can't escape *me!* I can *see* you!' By then I had my nose to the ground..."

"Not to the grindstone like you should have been!"

I ignored him and continued. "And then I was suddenly aware that if any of the neighbours saw me they would think I was having an excited conversation with the earth! There's no telling *what* they'd do!"

"Phone the men in their long white coats to come and take you away, ha ha! It'd be like that weird song that came out in the nineteen sixties...you know (and he added this part sing-song), they're coming to take me away, ha ha - to the *funny* farm, ha ha he he!"

"How do you know about *that?*"

"Must I remind you yet again that we have long, inherited memories? Anyway, we have spoken about this before and it was in relation to that awful man who used to visit us. Remember? The police took him away...to the funny farm, ha ha!"

No trace of his oft-used uncouth speech *there*.

"You have such a small head to be packing so much data into it!" I retorted. "Did you like the story about the crickets?"

"Yeah, but it took you a long time to tell it."

"That's because you jolly well kept interrupting me."

"Think I'll go and make a phone call."

"Who to?"

"The men at the funny farm, ha ha he heeee!"

Then he ran away sniggering, and almost on cue Katie appeared around the corner of the small courtyard, yawning as she so often did.

"Hello Mum. How have you been?"

"Fed up, dat's - I mean, *that's* what!"

"When will we be moving house?"

"Not for a few weeks. I have so much to do first. The major job is in finding us a decent place to live, somewhere not as cramped as this one."

"Oh good. We pussycats need our freedom."

"So do I, Katie O'Brien, so do I."

**

Reilly returned from having a drink - at least, I assumed that's what he'd been doing, and no doubt it was from the toilet again. I asked him.

"None of your business, woman."

"I never know how to take you, Reilly. You're so approachable sometimes, and other times you exasperate me so much I could...I could..."

"Throw me out on the streets? I would make you *pay!*"

"I have no doubts whatsoever about *that!*"

He turned to wash his rear.

"Hmmm," I added, remembering another amusing incident from the distant past. "Do you want to hear another story?"

"Not if it's going to portray you as a daft woman."

"No...this one is about a daft man."

"Okay, get on wid it."

Both he and Katie sat in the doorway, watching me in a most disconcerting manner.

"It happened some years ago...I was visiting my former husband's Uncle Calvin, a most eccentric man..."

"Runs in the family, huh?"

"No! He wasn't a blood relation...anyway, as I was saying, I was visiting him one day and he had this big cat there..."

"As big as me?"

"Possibly a bit bigger, Reilly. He was a big tabby..."

"Da uncle or da cat?"

"Stop interrupting me! I'm talking about the cat! Anyway, he'd named it Elsa, who was a stray. I asked him what made him think the cat was a girl?"

"It was da way she wriggled her rear!"

"Don't be rude, cat! No...Uncle Calvin replied that he felt it was far too improper a thing to do to such a dignified animal - as to go looking under its tail..."

"I should *think* so! If anyone looked under *my* tail I would make sure he didn't do *dat* ever again!"

"Anyway, on with the story. I had a quiet chuckle to myself at Uncle Calvin's attitude. 'Undignified it may seem, Uncle,' I'd said to him, 'but it's one way to find out for sure, whether she's an Elsa or an Ellis'. But just after that, "Elsa" turned and walked down the little garden path and I had to tell him: 'Uncle, Elsa is most definitely a boy!' What do you mean? he asked me. 'Owing to the fact that he could play ping-pong all by himself, with what was hanging out from under his tail', I said. Uncle Calvin thought that was *most* undignified!"

"Yeah, and so do I!"

"You wanted to hear the story," I reminded him.

"You are a rude woman, staring at dat tomcat's privates."

"I couldn't help it - they were so *huge!*"

"Oh my, my," breathed Katie, and Reilly looked daggers at her.

"Unfaithful little cat! How *dare* you drool over another cat!"

"Mum made him sound so, so *fascinating!*"

"I expect you to have eyes only for *me,* Katie O'Brien!"

"While *you* look at whatever girl pussycat you please!" she retorted.

"It's a man's world, and it wasn't me what first said dat, so you can't blame *me* for dat saying!" He turned to glare at me, his eyes half-closed, expecting me to rise to his bait.

"I didn't say you'd first said it. You swishing you tail like that reminds me of another story..."

He appeared to roll his eyes.

"Here we go again!"

"You don't have to hear it if you don't want to," I said huffily.

"On wid it den woman! Can't have you blubbing all over the place!"

"I was *not*, I repeat *not* blubbing! I *never* blub...except when there's a cute animal story on the telly..."

"You were saying?"

Both he and Katie were washing themselves and I thought I'd lost their attention, but as if on cue, they both stopped and gazed unblinkingly at me.

"Yes...well...when I was living in Nelson, I rescued this very pregnant little cat. She was so pretty and had such a personality..."

"We *all* have great personalities!" Reilly snapped.

"When will you learn to stop interrupting me?" I almost shouted.

"When it suits me," was the glib reply.

"Anyway, it still angers me when I discover abandoned cats... but Hoover was so pretty..."

"*Hoover?* What sort of a name was *dat?*"

"It's the name I gave her for the time being because of the way she sucked up food, poor thing. Making up for the food she'd missed out on. Besides, she liked the name. It gave her a feeling of importance."

"*Hoover?* Vacuum cleaner? I think not!"

"Think of the famous American, President Hoover."

"Yeah, blamed by many for the Great Depression."

"Whatever. Anyway, Hoover got fatter and fatter and by my reckoning, she was overdue with her kittens. So I took her to a vet, who cheerfully puffed away on his pipe while he examined her and said she was in fine fettle..."

"At least he didn't say she'd been in a good paddock, like that vet you took *me* to."

"Maybe not, but he probably meant the same. That wasn't a criticism Reilly...but back to the story. The vet I took Hoover to said that her kittens would be due in a few days' time and by the look and feel of her she'd have about ten kittens! I was still sure she was overdue and that there wouldn't be anywhere near that amount."

"So what happened?"

"She had just two, early the next morning, and the first one came out *purring.*"

"Really?"

"Yes, *really.*"

"Poor little sod, it was probably so grateful to be out of dat squashed space it couldn't help but purr."

"It was absolutely fascinating! And the second one purred too, although not as loudly. It was the funny crackling sound that woke me up."

"So after all dat, you were right and da vet was wrong, huh?"

"Yup," I said, grinning.

"Do you have to look so smug, woman?"

"Maybe it's cat-ching!" I retorted, eyeing him in what I hoped was a disarming manner.

"You're just a smart alec!"

"Like I said, it's cat-ching."

But Reilly had to go one better.

"I suppose you realize that all those stories portray human ignorance?"

"Of course I realize. I just wanted you to feel better about yourself!"

"I don't *need* to. It's humans who always have to justify their actions! Come on Katie O'Brien, let's go outside and find a place where there are few, or even *no* humans."

"Antarctica!" I called as they went outside.

"If dat's where you're going to jaunt off to next, you can count us out! We're not silly, you know."

"I never said you *were.*"

"I'm just making sure you understand dat point!" he called back, peering around the corner.

"Oh, I understand very well," I replied, incensed.

"In dat case, I'm just reiterating it," he smirked.

"There's that word again," I sighed.

Reilly gave a swish of his fluffy tail, chirruped at Katie and bounded into the courtyard to leap at a leaf blowing in the breeze, and then to leap at Katie and bite her.

"Ow! You beast, Reilly!"

"Gotta keep you women under control."

"Why?"

"Why? Because why is a crooked letter and zed is no better!"

"Reilly, sometimes I just don't understand you!" Katie piped angrily.

*Amen to that,* I thought.

\*\*\*

# CHAPTER TWENTY FIVE

## *On The Road Again*

My requirements for the right place for us were high by some standards: it must not be too expensive; it must have two bedrooms and be clean and must be in reasonable proximity to the Christchurch Star office. I answered numerous advertisements for houses and flats to rent but all of them had drawbacks; not only were they still too far away from the Star, but they weren't suitable in other aspects. Others, more suitable, stated, "no pets".

"Not even a pet snake? A well-behaved python?" I asked one prospective landlord who was already proving to be a not-so-nice person. He looked at me as if I was off my rocker, and said so.

"We writers are allowed to be eccentric," I said. "What's a snake or two between friends anyway?"

It was my way of getting back at a prospective landlord who made veiled suggestions about offering more than a flat to rent. The way he kept looking sideways at me and saying how nice it would be to have me next door was a pretty good hint too that he had more on his mind than what was proper. It didn't surprise me that I never heard from him again after mentioning pet pythons. That suited me just fine.

Just one week before the cats and I were due to move out of our temporary housing, I was driving down the scenic Heathcote valley, thinking how pretty it was at this time of year and wondering if I could find a new place to rent in time, and if it could have been in this area. I called up the rental agency for the third time that day and when the receptionist mentioned a townhouse in Linwood, my spirits lifted. Linwood didn't have the best reputation in the city for being the ideal suburb in which to live, but at least it was close to the Star and handy to the central city. After phoning the bubbly landlady, I was almost convinced the place was ideal.

"Don't take too much notice of my husband though dear. He can be a grumpy old bugger but don't let that put you off."

She was so friendly and cheerful I thought I could put up with any amount of grumpiness from her husband, if they decided I would be a suitable tenant.

When I walked up the clean and spacious driveway I knew this was the place for me and my cats, and I intended to pull out all stops to get it. The landlord was inside; a small, wiry man, he did sound grumpy but I was determined to show him I was capable of keeping up with rent payments and that I was indeed a busy journalist. I'd come prepared. I showed him one of my many scrapbooks so he could see for himself that I really did what I said. And that it was recent work.

To my enormous pleasure he accepted me and the cats, albeit grudgingly with the latter. When I explained that they were well looked after, both spayed and friendly, the landlord's voice went up an octave.

"As long as they don't go pooing and yowling around the place," he said briskly. I told him I'd make sure their behaviour was impeccable, and crossed my fingers behind my back. He gave a nod of grudging acceptance.

Moving day came and went smoothly. My friend Mike - another Mike whom I'd met through our association with the Star, came to see me when the removal men had left. I was busy unpacking crockery when he arrived, and offered him a cup of coffee but first had to find the mugs.

The cats were busy exploring the flat, taking great note of the smell left in a couple of corners by previous cat tenants. I got rid of the smell very promptly with strong disinfectant, and the cats soon found other things to interest them.

The divider at the end of the bath, for instance, was ideal for them to leap from, to land on the vanity unit. And they would leap back again. This provided a good pastime for them but it did have its hazards. It was disconcerting to say the least, to be busy washing one's hands when a cat chose that precise moment to fling himself or herself at you. Katie occasionally landed on my back; I considered it a blessing I had thus so far managed to step out of the way in time when Reilly tried the same. I shudder to think of the deep scratches in my back he would have made if he'd landed on his target, namely, me.

"You see, woman, I really am a most considerate cat, when all's said and done."

"I am so grateful," I said.

"I'm so glad you are."

His eyes were narrowed at me, suspecting sarcasm. I smiled and petted him, earning a swipe.

"Now cat, I have much to do - stories to write, deadlines to meet!"

As if on cue the telephone rang. I was almost wishing I hadn't had the phone connected for a few more days at least, to give me a rest after moving in. The phone call was from one of the advertising salesmen from the Star, asking me if I could write a thousand-word story at short notice. I agreed. And that's the way my life was set for the next two years - more deadlines than I'd ever had to deal with before, less sleep, more interviews to make with farmers from all over the country. Some of them were interviewed via telephone at 10pm, or early in the morning - whatever time was suitable for them.

One morning when I stumbled out of bed, exhausted, Reilly took one look at me and said: "dis is gettin' beyond a joke, woman! How can you take proper care of us when you look like a worn-out old dishrag?"

"Charming, very charming!" I said waspishly. "Have you and Katie gone without anything? Have you been underfed, lacked cuddles and attention or been left out in the frost?"

"No, no, no to all dat stuff. Even if I do say so myself, you are a good woman."

"Reilly!" I exclaimed with delight. "You love me after all!" I bent to cuddle them both and while Katie stayed in the circle of my arms, Reilly tried to wriggle free.

"Ergh! Gerroff!"

Still, it didn't matter that Reilly wriggled out of my arms. It was one of the rare times in his life he agreed that I wasn't so bad. High praise from Seamus O'Reilly, and that's a fact! My spirits were perked up no end, and I was able to race through that day's work.

**

It was my new friend Mike's birthday. I bought him a pair of smart black moccasin-style shoes and his family gave him clothing too, which he brought to my place to show off. He tried on the heavy-duty yellow PVC raincoat his mother had given him.

"Don't know if it'll be big enough fer me," he said in his strong Liverpudlian accent. At 6ft 3" and nearly 300lbs in weight, he's a very big man and dwarfed my small apartment. I helped him into the coat and had the feeling we were being watched. I turned to see Reilly sitting there on the sheepswool mat, grinning for all his worth. Except for his colouring, I was immediately put in mind of the Cheshire Cat.

Turning back to Mike, I helped him with the hood of the coat.

"He looks like a giant corncob," Reilly observed.

I laughed heartily.

"He does, too!"

"What?" Mike said, smiling but looking puzzled.

"Reilly said you look like a giant corncob."

"That's right! Blame the cat!"

"That's what he said," I insisted. I glanced over at Reilly, who was still sitting on the sheepswool mat, but this time he had a most innocent look on his handsome face. Katie, who had been sleeping on my bed, emerged yawning. It seems to me that that's a picture I often have in my mind, of Katie sleepily emerging, yawning and stretching and opening her big eyes wider. She took one look at Mike; this time her eyes seemed twice as big and she shot out the door, around the corner to the laundry and yowled to go outside.

"Looks like I scared yer other cat," Mike said with a grin. My stomach contracted with another urge to laugh, but I didn't want to hurt Mike's feelings.

"Okay Mike, model the coat for us," I said bossily, and Mike did just that, pirouetting around in my lounge room. The coat was tight across his tummy and despite Reilly's description of Mike being like a giant corncob, the coat suited him. But the huge man pirouetting in a bright yellow coat was too much for Reilly. He too, shot out to the small laundry and yowled to go outside.

Grinning broadly, I let them out; Katie shot off in one direction and Reilly made a beeline towards Mike's small blue car. Mike is one of those big men who, for some quirk of personality, choose to own small cars.

Reilly loved to get onto cars and investigate every panel, every nook and cranny and every lurking spider web attached to windscreen wipers and side mirrors. As soon as Reilly landed with a thud on the car, Mike's one-eyed black toy poodle/Maltese cross named Mickey was aroused from a nap.

"Arrgh! Yap yap!"

"Grrr. What's a small black one-eyed lamb doing sitting and bleating in a car?" Reilly sniggered.

"I am a full-grown toy poodle/Maltese cross, yap yap!"

"You lie through your teeth. Oh I see, you've hardly *got* any! Okay, I'll amend dat. You lie through your *tooth*."

"Yap yap!"

"Stop dat dreadful racket! Do you want the neighbours to complain? My person might get evicted!"

"Get off my human's car!"

"Certainly not! Dis is *my* territory and youse in it, Thingy - whatever youse are."

"I am a fine, upstanding *dog!*"

"A runty little black sheep, dat's what you are. Good for eating! Yum yum! Not as good as rabbit, but you'll do!"

Mickey leaped up and danced around furiously.

"Wait 'til I tell my human!"

"Tell him what? Dat youse on my territory? I should come right through dat window and gobble you up! I'm *hungry!*"

"I'm a *dog!*" Mickey yapped furiously.

"And I'm hungry and youse is a runty sheep! Probably a bit tough, but never mind, I like a good chew now and den."

"Go away! Go away!" Mickey screamed.

"What a nasty temper! Grrr!"

"Grr, yap yap!"

Mike, who had been busy modeling the yellow coat and wondering where he could wear it, came rushing outside to see what all the commotion was about.

I always step aside when big Mike comes rushing.

Reilly looked up innocently as we approached the car, while Mickey continued to leap about.

"Why, if it ain't dat giant corncob again, dis time on da move. Now dat *is* a scary sight!"

"Get off the car, Reilly," I said.

"Dat black runty sheep is being inhospitable to me, woman. Dis is *my* territory, after all!"

"Mickey only wants to play," said Mike.

"Oh yeah? I think he'd like to *kill* me, but he'd have to *gum* me to death, ha ha!"

"Reilly, that's not very nice," I said while I pulled him off the car. He resisted and growled at me.

"What?" asked Mike. "What did you say?"

"I was talking to Reilly. Gosh his language deteriorates when he's defending his territory!"

"Right," Mike replied with a grin and a small shake of his head.

**

# TERRITORIAL FRIGHTS.....

"DON'T GET UNRAVELLED — ALL I SAID WAS
YOU LOOK LIKE A BALL OF STRING!"

It was a glorious autumn day, late afternoon. Katie was doing the sensible thing - exploring the garden while Reilly was sound asleep on the cream velvet sofa I'd recently bought. He looked so wonderful with the sun's rays shafting across him that he seemed too handsome to be real. His twitching while he was asleep told otherwise. I wondered what he dreamed about. Did he dream of revenge or the only slightly-lesser term of getting even? Or did he, by a stretch of my imagination, dream of ways to please me?

A man by the name of W.H. Auden said cats can be very funny and have the oddest ways of showing they're pleased to see you. "Rudimace always peed in our shoes," he said. Fortunately that never happened with me. Both cats had always been good in their personal habits and the only thing that got me running in the middle of the night was the "whoop whoop" sound when one of my cats was being sick. But that was rare and usually a dose of some form of fish oil was enough to clear their systems of hair balls or other matter. Their health is excellent, maintained by a good diet, plenty of exercise and affection, and regular vaccinations.

As I watched him sleeping and twitching in his sleep, I wondered also, if he dreamed of the great outdoors again, stealing through the shadows after prey, real or imaginary.

### *Night Reilly*

When the fading day's hush
whispers to the birds
that the long day is done
and a last skylark call is heard;

when the silver-grey cat
complete with his white mask
slinks through the undergrowth
and takes lingering ants to task;

when the cool evening's shimmer
of a memory-filled breeze
taunts the cat into wariness
and he lowers into the grass with ease;

that's when the owl calls
in his comical, yet haunting way
and Reilly pauses, expectant,
and heralds the close of day;

he welcomes the velvet of night
where ancient cat-memory lies,
and with every breeze caressing him,
with absolute pleasure the cat relaxes and sighs.

*The day is long done:*
*a fresh new evening has begun.*

\*\*

I wrote that poem while I watched him, imagining what *he* might be imagining.

Suddenly, as if aware of my scrutiny, Reilly woke up and stared at me.

"Well?"

"Well what?"

"Why are you staring at me like dat?"

"I was just thinking about our good times together and what you might have been dreaming about."

"We've done a lot, haven't we? Haven't I been a good cat!"

"Not always," I grinned. "But life sure hasn't been dull without you and Katie around."

"So your good life is all due to me, huh?"

"Yeah, all due to Reilly...not forgetting wee Katie, of course."

"I s'pose not."

I looked at him consideringly. Was that vital spark of his growing dull or was that my imagination? "You're *happy* here aren't you?"

"I wanna go back to the West Coast."

"I thought you liked it here and were happy to stay?"

"Yeah it's okay...but it's the call of the wild, you know?"

"I understand, cat. Someday we will - when I don't have to meet all these deadlines anymore - when I can just sit back and write other stories."

"You'd still be writing."

"Of a far more creative sort, my dear cat."

He yawned and stretched. "You promised another six months here on this side of the island, but it's stretched to over two years! Huh! Think I'll go outside and see what Katie's up to."

"As long as you don't pick on her."

Reilly appeared to smile. The spark was back again. "Would I do dat?"

"Yes you would."

"I am grievously stricken!" he declared unconvincingly.

"I'm sure!" I retorted.

"Haven't I been a continuous answer to prayer? Remember those years ago when you prayed for a tough tomcat?"

"Oh, I remember well," I replied, smiling.

Just then the lark, high in the sky began singing his piercingly sweet song. It was as if he was putting his seal on the end of the glorious autumn day.

"Didn't you claim God's promise to supply every need?"

"I did, and I thanked Him for them," I replied, my smile broadening.

"Well then, I was your *need.* You lucky woman - you got *me.*"

"Amen to that too," I laughed.

\*\*\*


THE END

*All Due To Reilly*
*Amber Jo Illsley © 2015*

This is the second in a series about author Amber Jo Illsley's cat Reilly...in full: Seamus O'Reilly. A semi-fictional, illustrated story, Reilly continues his antics and witty repartee with the author, inviting occasional interjections from the sleepy and long-suffering Katie O'Brien, Reilly's girlfriend.

"All Due To Reilly" covers several years in which the author and her cats move to several different addresses, mainly to do with the course of the author's work. The big move from west to east and then to Switzerland, for the author at least, incurs recriminations and the subsequent disappearance of Reilly - only for him to reappear months later to resume his lofty household position.

This new story brings the reader up to present times in Reilly's life and misdemeanours.

**

Printed in the United States
By Bookmasters